Sarah, opening her eyes, looked at Magdalene, whose eyes were closed. Sarah took a deep breath. Another. The resounding pulse within her was beginning to soften. Energy was running through her from head to toe like a spring river. Magdalene opened soft eyes and slowly connected with Sarah's. A sprite suddenly danced within their glance. Fairies of dust and lust sprinkled their work all through the air. And the devil of dare perched on Magdalene's shoulder. Magdalene ventured, "Sarah, may I ask you a personal question?"

Sarah affirmed with her eyes.

"What do you like?" Magdalene dared one step closer.

"What do you mean?" Sarah looked directly at Magdalene.

A dangerous smile infiltrated Magdalene's visage. Her eyebrows raised ever so slightly and her mouth opened slowly. "You like to be on top, don't you?"

Magdalene took hold of Sarah's other wrist to check the pulse as Sarah asked, "And you, what do you like?"

Magdalene leaned closely to her and said with sultry confidentiality, "I like to talk dirty. And I like to be on the bottom."

Meltdown. Sarah met her match. Her body smiled.

About the Author

Marilyn Freeman lives in Olympia with her partner, Carol, two dogs, and a cat. Originally from Spokane, Marilyn graduated from the Cornish College of the Arts in Seattle with a Bachelor of Fine Arts in Theatre. She lived in Manhattan for ten years, worked primarily in television, and moved back to the Northwest (1991) where she has been answering the call to write and make films. She started Olympia Pictures, produced and directed *In My Father's Bed* (1993), *American Values* (1994), and wrote and directed *Meeting Magdalene* (1995), which was first a film. Visit the Olympia Pictures web site at http://www.olympiapix.com.

Meeting Magdalene

by Marilyn Freeman

THE NAIAD PRESS, INC.
1997

Copyright © 1997 by Marilyn Freeman

All rights reserved. No part of this book may be reproduced or transmitted in any form or by any means, electronic or mechanical, including photocopying, without permission in writing from the publisher.

Printed in the United States of America on acid-free paper
First Edition

Editor: Lisa Epson
Cover designer: Bonnie Liss (Phoenix Graphics)
Typesetter: Sandi Stancil

Library of Congress Cataloging-in-Publication Data

Freeman, Marilyn, 1954 –
   Meeting Magdalene / by Marilyn Freeman.
      p.   cm.
   ISBN 1-56280-170-8
   I. Title.
PS3556.R3923M44   1996
813'.54—dc21   96-46883
                                                                                          CIP

To
*Vi & Ken, Patt, Tomm & Kenny
with whom life began*

Acknowledgments

I am grateful to many individuals who support my writing and filmmaking in different ways. I wish to acknowledge here a few extraordinary women who have been most significant in the process of writing this collection:

Carol Hamilton, my amazing friend and partner, whose love, spirit, and humor make my life richer than I ever imagined, and whose Cancer nature keeps my Scorpio madness almost manageable;

Lynn Damiano, my adventure guide, who walked me through the valley of darkness and up the mountain of need to the summit of vulnerability and trust;

Gina Largent, my erudite, generous new friend, who in the midst of changing jobs and moving made time to read my work, give insightful edits and inspiring critiques;

Stephanie Kaye, my lifelong, magical and gifted friend, for her endlessly creative and increasingly courageous spirit, tough and detailed critiques, and high expectations; and

Lizzy Kaye, my longtime friend and creative coconspirator, who played the lead in my first film, reads with impassioned interest everything I write, and graces my work with her brilliant sense of art and character.

Contents

Have You Got a Problem with That? 1

In the Way of Intimacy 33

Bellevue Housewives 59

Before Dawn 85

Meeting Magdalene 95

Have You Got a Problem with That?

"I can accept it, but I can't condone it." That was how Esther Jewell reconciled her daughter's lifestyle. Esther was retired, a smoldering fireball at sixty-five, intimidating in her stoicism. Her hazel eyes looked more inward than outward. She'd shrunk from five-foot-five-inches to five-foot-three: osteoporosis, never was one to exercise. Drank a pot of coffee a day, percolated, for some fifty years. She'd long ago forgotten exactly when that bunion on her right foot started. Esther was one of those women who worked her whole life. Always employed, worked because she had to. Her husband, who'd died three years earlier, never could keep a job. Esther, however, was steadfast: a veteran law-office bookkeeper; the breadwinner and the bread maker. She had three kids to raise and made sure they had a decent home, clean clothes, and plenty of food.

The oldest child was Mya who had stayed in Spokane, Esther's hometown. Mya was a part-time cosmetics distributor and full-time born-again Christian. Esther's only son, Don, had died in Vietnam. One of Esther's nephews, Steven, had grown to be somewhat of a surrogate son. His parents had died his last year in high school; Esther took him in. He was the same age Don would have been. Steven had gone to law school in Oregon and settled in Lebanon, a small town there. Though he always kept a personal distance he faithfully visited and called Esther like a dutiful child. Then there was Jenelle, Esther's youngest daughter. She was ten years younger than Mya, and eight years younger than Steven. Right after college, Jenelle had gone off to the big city: New York.

Esther was Catholic, and considered herself devout. She'd sent all of her kids to Catholic schools. Went to mass every Sunday of her life, even when she was on vacation. Retirement afforded her time to attend early morning masses on weekdays at the Poor Clares' chapel. Though Esther never got involved with the Parent Teacher Associations, or her kids' athletic programs, or any other extracurricular activities, she always paid special attention to the Poor Clares, a cloistered order of nuns dedicated to prayer. No one ever saw them: they lived behind walls, curtains, and screens. A fifteen-foot-tall concrete wall covered with small stones enclosed the Poor Clares. Esther always personally delivered pies and cakes she'd made during the holidays specially for them. She had no interest in any other order of nuns. Certainly not the ones who ran her kids' schools, the Holy Name nuns. "If they think for one minute that I wouldn't join the PTA, and do cakewalks, and doughnut socials, and all their other crap if I didn't have to work, well then — they've got another think coming." But those cloistered nuns were another story. "There are days when I think I could have been a Poor Clare," Esther said periodically over the years.

It was a muggy day in the middle of June 1987 when twenty-nine-year-old Jenelle met Esther at LaGuardia Airport in New York City. Jenelle Kayla Jewell. The most beautiful name in the world, Esther thought. This was her first visit to see Jen in the five years she'd lived in Manhattan.

Jen was always intensely spirited. She was the one who was held after school for bad behavior, for writing graffiti on the board during recess: love notes like BOB LOVES PEGGY; political messages like SISTER BEATRICE IS FAR OUT. Once she was detained after school for setting off the fire alarm. She was supposed to ring the bell signaling the end of recess but accidentally rang the alarm. Sister Superior burst out of her third-grade class as if she'd been struck with nuclear diarrhea. All the nuns went wild, stricken with fear, black-and-white penguins racing about the halls towering over confused kids. Seeing the nuns go absolutely mad for some five minutes made Jen's weeklong detention worth it.

At the end of her third decade Jen maintained a fine physique: a hard body, medium build with well-defined arms, strong legs, and a deliciously flat stomach. She had wavy, blond hair with a mind of its own and bright blue eyes faster than a humming-bird. Her Buddy Holly black-framed glasses distinguished her as more urban than suburban.

Jen was ambitious. She worked hard as a freelance writer. Landed lots of writing gigs: newsletters and brochures for companies, copy for ad agencies, on-air promotional spots for fledgling cable networks, an occasional magazine article. If she hit a dry spell she'd do pro bono flyers for the neighborhood deli or dry cleaner or rewrite her own promotional brochure.

She lived in a tiny studio apartment on Twentieth Street in Chelsea. The smallest living space Esther had ever seen. The place had more room going up than across. The twelve-foot-high ceiling created enough height for a built-in loft. It held Jen's mattress — a futon, Esther learned the thing was called. There was enough room under the loft for a small television set and a foam-filled love seat that made into a bed. Between the loft and the interior apartment wall was a narrow, four-foot-long wood table: Jen's desk, painted purple. Purple bookshelves ran up the wall on tracks above the desk, beside the loft, all the way to the ceiling. Dr. Seuss and New Age, self-help books populated the shelves. Titles commingled: *The Art of You, Green Eggs and Ham,*

Whose Life Are You Living?, *A Course in Miracles*, *How the Grinch Stole Christmas*, and *Stop Smoking with the Power of Crystals*.

There was one window, four-foot-wide and eight-foot-high, reaching up into the loft. The apartment looked out onto an Episcopal seminary across the street that occupied a full city block. The monastery grounds were quite parklike, an environmental anomaly in that metropolis, and a big reason Jen elected to live there. "A church! Now that's nice," Esther had said, glad there was some kind of house of God nearby, even if it wasn't Catholic.

Jen dragged Esther all over Manhattan during their ten-day visit. They ate cold noodles with sesame sauce in Chinatown. Had cannolis in Little Italy. Sipped cappuccino in Soho. Feasted on bagels and chopped liver at Barney Greengrass's on the Upper West Side. Rode a hansom cab through Central Park. Indulged in high tea at the Plaza Hotel. Bought show tickets in Times Square. Saw *Cats* at the Wintergarten Theater on Broadway. Got into a live taping of the "David Letterman Show" in the NBC Building at Rockefeller Center. Strolled Tiffany's and Saks and F.A.O. Schwarz on Fifth Avenue. Browsed the souvenir shop in St. Patrick's Cathedral. And on the eighth day, after seeing *Hannah and Her Sisters* at the Greenwich Theater, stumbled into the gay pride parade in the West Village; it was a scene.

Esther was all eyes. While Jen maneuvered them toward some possibility of a cab, Esther watched more of the parade on the sidewalk than in the street. Men in dresses, men in briefs, men in thongs. And the women! Big, small, and very big. Fierce, hairy, and often tattooed. Men and women alike; all wearing something akin to army boots. Leather galore: around necks, wrists, and torsos. Leather chaps, leather pants, leather jackets, even in the heat of June.

They made their way through the festive throngs of Christopher street. "Well, I think I'm ready to go home," Esther said without direct comment on the sights, though her eyes darted wildly from one spectacle to the next. Jen guessed Esther meant home to Spokane, not her apartment. A group of ten or so women with a pack of wiener dogs approached. They buoyed signs, even though they were no longer in the official parade, that read WOMEN WITH WEENIES. Esther smiled completely unintentionally.

She clasped her purse closer as a contingent of very tall men, like a party of poplar trees, engulfed them. They wore gigantic wigs, heavy blue eye shadow, broom-sized lashes, skyscraper stilettos, and extra-large leotards bearing Miss Universe banners with the names of various states. Miss Oregon fixed directly on Esther, then flashed a big, beauty-princess smile, "Oh, Mom! You're here!" stretching out his arms to Esther.

Esther's eyes bugged. She jerked a look over her sagging shoulder as if to verify he wasn't talking to her. Jen gave Miss Oregon a pantomimed plea for a break. The towering Miss Maine curtsied. Jen smiled on behalf of her mother. Miss Oregon gave a princess wave, "Have a nice day, Mom!" Finally, Jen escorted Esther out of the gender-twisting pageant.

"Let's go to the Empire Diner for dinner tonight," Jen said, flagging cabs on Seventh Avenue with no luck. "I'm sorry, Mom, I think we're going to have to walk a little farther." Esther, like a soldier, trooped on.

"We could just go to your apartment and fix dinner there," Esther said flatly, still guarding her purse, perspiration gathering in the frowning lines of her face.

"Come on, Mom, you spent enough of your life cooking. Let me take you out," Jen said mustering lightheartedness, not looking at Esther. Jen closed her eyes momentarily trying to diffuse the inevitable strain from her mother's visit.

"I've eaten out more in the last eight days than I have in the last eight years," Esther said with a hint of disgust.

"I'm sorry, Mom. I thought it would be fun for you to eat out and stuff," Jen said trying to remain pleasant. She searched again for a cab.

"It is fun. It's just so expensive. You've been shoveling out money ever since I got here."

"Mom, this is New York," Jen said condescendingly, revealing the attitude of a big-city chauvinist. "That's what you do here. You shovel out money."

"Maybe they ought to try shoveling a little something else out of here," Esther sparred, eyeing a middle-aged, big-bellied man in leather briefs with daisy pasties on his nipples.

"Mom," Jen said, eyeing her eyeing him, in a tone of please-don't-start.

"I could make something nice for dinner at your place tonight." Esther put on her pleasant voice.

Jen dodged a man on roller blades wearing a fairy princess tutu. "Okay, but tomorrow night we're having dinner out with Fran. I want to you to meet her."

Esther made spaghetti later that night. She added sautéed onion and green pepper to some bottled sauce. Jen was reminded how her mother could make anything taste great. They ate and talked about Mya, her husband, Ralph, and their son, Joe. Ralph was also born-again. Joe was in his third year studying architectural lighting at the California College of Arts and Crafts. Joe told his Aunt Jen he was glad to be far from home. Since finishing high school he'd gone back home only for short visits. Joe had never shown an interest in girls, always preferred boys. Mya and Ralph prayed for his redemption regularly, including times when he was home visiting. That night over dinner, Jen and Esther stuck to safe topics: Ralph's construction company, Joe's career ambitions, and Mya's cosmetics business. They also talked about Steven and his law practice. Nothing was discussed about colliding with the gay pride festivities earlier that day.

Jen looked with hope at every romantic relationship: that it may be the big one. So it was important to her that Esther meet Fran, even though Jen had been seeing Fran barely two months. Fran was a nurse who worked at the Soho Clinic on Spring Street. Fran's eccentricities were not apparent on the surface. Jen had been ignoring the oddities that appeared, usually manifesting in Fran's diverse collection of friends. Had Jen been a little more realistic in her assessment of Fran, Jen might have been better prepared for when Fran met Esther the next night as planned.

It was Esther's last night in town — fiasco at the Cottonwood Café. An old friend of Fran's appeared at the table just as their pork chops and mashed potatoes with gravy arrived. The friend was dressed in flaming dominatrix attire: fishnet stockings; high, high spiked heels; a very tight, black leather halter, miniskirt, and cop-style cap. Wielding a whip, she led two women on leashes. One, very tall, very thin. Very handcuffed. The other, very demure, very obsequious. Very all over the diva.

Jen tried to make her nervous chuckle a blasé laugh of indifference. Esther was not amused. Jen suffered an acute nicotine fit and wished she hadn't stopped smoking the year before. "What time will we need to leave for the airport in the morning?" Esther asked, dismissing the exchange between Fran and her friends.

All the bagels, historical sights, special shows, and shopping seemed to vanish from Esther's recall, replaced only by the menacing memory of gay pride and dinner with Fran. Esther got on the Spokane-bound plane without a smile, disturbed. Shortly after that visit Esther came down with gout in her right foot, apparently from all the city walking. Add that to the bunion of many years and she was left with quite a limp. She was never able to venture through New York the same way again.

Jen usually called Esther every Sunday evening. She continued to do so after Esther returned to

Spokane that time, but they never did discuss her visit.

"I had lunch with Mabel on Wednesday," Esther had said one Sunday night a couple of months later. "No, wait, I guess that was Tuesday. That's right, it was Tuesday because I played pinochle on Wednesday."

"Uh huh," Jen automatically replied. Then she made a stab at telling Esther something that was really on her mind, her heart beating like a propeller. "Fran and I broke up, Mom."

Pause.

Jen continued, "I wasn't really expecting it, ya know."

Pause.

"Did I tell you Denny Harpman passed away?" Esther said without compunction.

Pause.

"Who's Denny Harpman?" Jen politely though resentfully obliged.

So it went. Jen went home for a few days at Christmas time. She cleaned Esther's garage, as she did each time she went home. Sat with Esther for hours and looked through old photos. Made the routine after-Christmas shopping rounds with Esther for wrapping paper, ribbons, and bows. And complied with visits to see Mya, in spite of Mya's obsessions with Christ and Mary Kay cosmetics.

"Praise the Lord, you look so . . . so healthy, Jenelle," Mya said, giving Jen a hint of an embrace by leaning toward her and patting her shoulder. "Doesn't Jenelle look . . . strong, Ralph?"

"Good to see you, Jenelle," Ralph joined in. "The Lord's been good to you, we hear."

"How's Joe?" Jen quickly asked about their overly artistic son. Jen never wasted any time bringing his name up when visiting her sister. Jen enjoyed letting Mya and Ralph know that she was very comfortable with Joe.

"Well, he's in our prayers, Jenelle," Mya always furrowed her brow when she spoke about their only child. "And you know, we've had concerns about his being in that San Francisco area because, well, because he's still at that age where he can be easily influenced."

"Yeah, cities are dangerous," Jen said nodding her head as if deadly serious. "And very queer as well." Jen was impatient, yet savvy, dealing with her sister's attitudes.

Ralph cocked an eye at Mya, as if to watch for her reaction to Jen's comment. Mya seemed not to have heard it, "Jen, I know you don't like makeup, but you really should try this new lipstick we carry. It's very subtle," Mya said, reaching for her sales supplies. Jen resigned herself with a sigh, and Esther pulled a wrinkled tissue from her sleeve and blew her nose into it.

Esther made her next New York visit the following October. It was 1988. By then Esther had sold her home and moved into Mya's house. Jen had moved to the Upper West Side of Manhattan and was living with Cindy: an attorney, about Jen's height, very thin, wavy brown hair with lots of body, gentle brown eyes. She spared no expense on clothes: a penchant for Comme des Garçons. She specialized in prenuptial agreements, divorces, and wills. Their romance, though not particularly passionate, had been swift.

"Let's throw caution to the wind and get an apartment together," Cindy invited one Sunday morning after reading the *New York Times*'s Metropolitan Diary aloud.

"I don't know if I can give up my Chelsea phone booth," Jen said jokingly. She'd lived in the tiny room for three years and was ready for a move. The thought of a grand apartment far outshadowed the implications of living with someone for the first time. So it was that August of 1988 they rented a spacious, two-bedroom condominium on Columbus Avenue. They put up six thousand dollars to get it: two thousand a month rent, two thousand for security deposit, two thousand for the last month's rent.

Jen knew she'd made a mistake within a week of moving in with Cindy. Whatever passion had been there vanished. Cindy immediately began putting in more hours at the office, often working Saturdays and Sundays. Time together disappeared. Within a couple of weeks, Jen began to realize the problem. It was Cindy's parents. Jen had never met them, though they lived in the suburbs of New York. Jen was happy when Cindy first announced she wanted to invite them over for dinner. But then she was utterly shocked.

"Listen," Cindy said in a businesslike way, "I want to close the door to the second bedroom and tell them that's your room."

"What?" Jen was appalled.

"They want to see the apartment," Cindy suddenly sounded like a detached Realtor.

Jen breathed deeply to stay calm, then said, "Cindy, you have to be honest with them."

"I can't tell them. It would kill them." Cindy absolutely dismissed the idea.

"If that's the way you have to deal with it, fine. But I'm not going to hang out and pretend I'm *just* a new *friend*." Jen was hurt and angry.

"Actually, it would probably be better if you're not here, anyway." Cindy was composed, matter-of-fact, and unaffected by Jen's emotional reaction.

Weirdness on Columbus Avenue. Jen had left her cozy, closet-sized Chelsea apartment to embark on a creepy adventure in someone else's closet-sized life. Cindy. Some model of success. Now what? Relocating was difficult and expensive in New York City. So they began couple's counseling. Jen had already made plans for Esther to come. She didn't want to cancel. How could she ever explain all this to Esther?

Esther was both intimidated and impressed by Jen's apartment building. The lobby struck Esther like that of a fancy hotel. The doorman especially daunted her: opening the door, greeting her by name, carrying even the smallest bag, signaling the elevator for her. Since she was quite lame from her damaged foot, she and Jen stayed in through most of her weeklong stay. On four of the days when Jen went to work, Esther read her Toni Morrison novel *Beloved*. Cindy was barely around during Esther's visit.

"I guess Cindy doesn't care for me," was Esther's summary of the situation to Jen as they sipped coffee together at the dining table.

"No, Mom, Cindy likes you. You know, she's a

lawyer. She's busy." Jen's mind flooded with things she wished she could tell Esther about her relationship with Cindy.

"The lawyers I worked for were never that busy," Esther said as she methodically smoothed her paper napkin next to her coffee mug.

"This is New York, Mom. It's different here."

"Yes, that it is," Esther said with no argument. Then she changed subjects, "So, you haven't told me about your visit with Steven."

"Oh, well, it was great, but I hardly saw him. He was here for some conference... stayed at the Hyatt in Times Square."

"Oh, so he stayed in a hotel," Esther said with disappointment in her voice.

"Yeah, but I met him twice for dinner. And he got to meet Cindy, too; they really hit it off." Then Jen hastened to add, "Both being lawyers, you know." Jen tried to qualify that so Esther wouldn't feel worse about Cindy's lack of interest in visiting. "It was nice to spend a little time with him, but he's hard to get to know, don't you think?" Jen and Steven were never very close, he was so much older, and very removed, kind of a loner. Even when Steven lived with them after his parents died, and Jen was just a little kid, he was very private.

"Well, I'm just glad the two of you hooked up while he was here. I got a card from him; he must have written it just after seeing you. He said he was very impressed with you," Esther glowed. Jen smiled. Esther went on, "I am very proud of you, Jen." Jen grinned as her mother beamed. Jen's career was going very well. She was on-air promotions manager for a new movie channel. Her time freelancing had paid off. "Your home is just lovely." Esther was somewhat awed at Jen's apparent success.

"It's a far cry from that puny little box in Chelsea, isn't it?" Jen said with a chuckle.

"I liked that apartment," Esther said pleasantly. "I liked that neighborhood. I like all those antique stores on Eighth Avenue."

Jen had no idea Esther paid that much attention to her old neighborhood. "I liked that neighborhood, too, Mom." She looked out at Columbus Avenue from the fifth-floor window thinking of the mess she was in with Cindy, and swallowed a cry. "I think I'm more of a downtown person."

"Well, maybe you'll live down there again. You never know." Esther's voice was comforting to Jen.

Nearly two years later, Esther came for her third visit. Jen was living downtown. And this time, Jen was in love. A whirlwind affair had ensued with the new programming manager for the music channel that Jen's company owned. The two channels had offices in the same building on Fifty-Ninth Street. Lisa was from California. Seven years younger than Jen, sandy-blond hair, wide-open hazel eyes. She walked like a cheerleader, had legs like a dancer and skin like a baby. She was very focused. In a soft sort of way. Very driven. In a quiet sort of way. She got what she wanted. In her own sort of way. She wanted Jen.

"Look," Lisa said, strolling into Jen's office one Friday afternoon. She wore a short denim skirt, faded-blue Converse All Stars, white socks. A button-down shirt, unbuttoned to the middle of her chest, revealing a tight-fitting man's sleeveless undershirt. "I've got to do the Women in Cable conference week after next in Chicago. You goin'?"

Jen watched as Lisa took up residency in the chair across the desk. "Not this year," Jen said, smiling, feeling that Lisa was flirting, but thinking that couldn't be true.

"Aw, come on. Why don't you go?" Lisa *was* flirting.

Jen couldn't quite believe it. "There are too many men at the Women in Cable deals," Jen explained her reason for not going, but was distracted by the uncontrollable urge to smile.

"Too many men, hmmm," Lisa acted like she was mulling this over as she picked up a rubber band from Jen's desktop. "Well, I've never gone before. I think you should go; it could be fun," Lisa smiled and shot the rubber band lightly at Jen.

Jen caught it, smiling. "You say that only because you haven't gone before." Jen shot it back at Lisa, "It'll be boring."

Lisa let it hit her and fall to the floor. Her vision was filled with Jen, "It won't be boring, I promise you." Lisa connected directly with Jen's eyes, heart and soul in one fell swoop.

"Okay," Jen surrendered, leaning back in her chair. Delighted. "Okay, I'll go."

They rented an apartment together one month after they got back from Chicago.

The stock market had crashed that last year, so apartments were available everywhere. They rented a duplex in the West Village: two bedrooms, fireplace, balcony, view of the Hudson and the Empire State

Building. All for sixteen hundred dollars a month, a deal by New York standards.

Jen could hardly wait for Esther to meet Lisa that June of 1990. They met Esther at the airport. Esther was pleasant. Lisa was pleasant. Together, Jen and Lisa took a couple of days off to spend with Esther during the week. After seven days, Jen finally broached with Esther a special outing Jen had been hesitant to bring up.

"So, Mom, a couple of friends of ours are getting married on Saturday. You wanna go to the wedding with us?" Jen forced a tone of casual conversation.

"Who is it? Anyone I know?" Esther asked nonchalantly without interrupting her knitting.

"No, you don't know them." Jen pushed her glasses up the bridge of her nose. Her voice went just a little higher than usual, "It's Sharon and Katherine." Jen looked quickly without meaning to at Lisa.

"Sharon and Katherine." Esther smiled as if she'd misunderstood. Looking at Jen, "You're joking."

"Uh, no," Jen said slowly, looking up from the floor to Esther. "I'm not joking."

"Two women?" Esther did not hide her astonishment.

"Yes," Jen resented her mother's reaction, though it came as no surprise.

"And they're getting married?" Esther asked in a tone that reminded Jen of getting caught skipping school.

"Yes, they're getting married at St. John's," Jen spoke with controlled calm. She was ashamed that she found it hard to bring the subject up to her mother. Ashamed that, like it or not, she too was uncomfortable with the idea that two women would get married. And she was angry that it was an issue in the first place.

"Two women are getting married in a church?" Esther went on almost as if she were enjoying a spectacle.

"Yeah," Jen felt dizzy, like she might pass out. "It's an Episcopal Church uptown."

"Oh, well, that explains it," Esther snapped with arrogance.

"Explains what?" Jen snapped back, fighting for consciousness.

Esther retreated with an indignant tone. "I think you girls should go without me."

Pause.

"All right." Jen resigned, and that was the end of that. Upon returning from the ceremony on Saturday, Esther asked nothing about it. Jen and Lisa volunteered that it was quite lovely. They did not mention they thought it was very strange that the two women had worn identical white dresses and said identical vows to each other. "What's up with the femmie Bobbsey Twins thing?" Jen whispered to Lisa during the service.

On the following day, Sunday, after a late breakfast of bagels and coffee at home, Jen mustered up the courage to present another foreign subject. "Mom, I'd really like to take you to a P-FLAG meeting this afternoon." Lisa looked up from her coffee without lifting her head, glancing first at Jen, then, at Esther.

"P — what?" Esther asked for clarification.

"P-FLAG," Jen said, folding the Arts and Leisure section with acute self-consciousness. "Parents and

Friends of Lesbians and Gays," Jen said and pressed her lips together tightly then released them trying desperately to relax.

"More coffee?" Lisa offered uncontrollably. She stood up; ready to exit.

"No, thanks," Esther said firmly.

"Yes, please," Jen said a little too loudly, glancing at Lisa, giving her the half-full Twin Peaks mug. Lisa bolted. "It's a really wonderful group," Jen continued, unconsciously biting her lip. "Ya know, it's mostly parents. They meet every fourth Sunday at a church in the neighborhood." Jen figured Esther wouldn't give the church angle much credence after the previous day's wedding announcement, but mentioned it nonetheless.

Esther sighed. "Why don't you girls go ahead without me?" She sounded tired, Jen knew this wasn't easy for her mother.

"Mom, I know you're not too keen on groups —" Jen acknowledged, then Esther interrupted.

"No, I'm not, Jen." The conversation made Esther visibly irritated.

Jen went on gently. "But I really want to introduce you to this organization." Jen watched her mother look away, out the window. Jen kept trying to engage her. "They have chapters all over the country, and I'm sure there's one in Spokane."

Esther said nothing; it was as though she'd left the room.

"Come on, Mom. This is important. I know you'd like this organization if you'd just give it a chance," Jen tried to reason.

"What makes you think so?" Esther asked, turning to Jen with a twinge of anger in her voice.

"Because they're really good people just like you, Mom." Jen nodded her head affirmingly, thinking she was on the right track. "And it would help give you some language for talking about me to your friends and the rest of the family."

"What's that supposed to mean?" Esther straightened up as if she were about to have a showdown with her boss.

Jen began to question Esther with hopes of enlightening her. "Well, what do you tell, I don't know, your friend Mabel when she asks about me?"

"I tell her how successful you are," Esther said without a second thought.

"Do you tell her about Lisa?" Jen asked, trying to clarify her point.

"No, I don't," Esther didn't hesitate.

"Well, why not?" Jen asked simply, without accusation.

"Because for all I know next month it won't be Lisa. It'll be Sue or Fran or Cindy," Esther spoke straight from her heart, her voice filled with both judgment and concern.

Jen looked down at her feet, stunned by her mother's frankness. Lisa walked back into the living room with Jen's coffee. Jen looked up, reassured by Lisa's presence, then ventured another question. "What do you say when people ask if I'm married yet?"

"I tell them no." Esther was never short on conviction.

Jen pursued the subject, "Do you tell them I'm not going to get married? At least not the way they think?"

"No, I tell them you just haven't met the right man yet," Esther said easily with a smile and lilt as if reciting an often-run commercial.

"Is that what you think?" Jen was annoyed, feeling the brunt of Esther's sudden levity.

"I don't know what to think," Esther's irritation returned.

"Will you please let me take you to this meeting, Mom," Jen pleaded. "I think it'll help you."

"I really don't want to go to some meeting, Jen. And I don't think I'm the one who needs the help."

"Okay, that's it. Lisa, let's go for a walk." Jen stood up and said to Esther, "Stay here if you like. But I'm not gonna sit here with you."

"Jen...?" Lisa said Jen's name as if to say, You sure you want to walk out like this?

"Lisa, let's go," Jen said with steaming firmness.

When they returned that evening Esther was already in bed. Her plane was leaving the next day, late in the morning. Jen took Esther to the airport and didn't say a word the whole way. Looked out her window from the torn vinyl backseat of the yellow cab. As they drove across the Williamsburg Bridge, Esther put her hand on Jen's. Jen pulled away.

Three Sundays went by without Jen calling Esther. On the fourth Sunday, Esther called Jen. "I have something to tell you," Esther said with emotion straining her voice. "Steven has AIDS."

"What?" Jen was shocked.

"Steven has AIDS," Esther said softly.

Jen sat down. "Steven?" Jen suddenly understood what motivated Steven's lifelong secrecy, why he never talked about his personal life, why conversation always focused on his career. Sadness swept through her. Tears automatically welled in her eyes. She took off her glasses, wondering how she could have been so completely out of touch with him, in every way. After his visit they'd exchanged holiday cards. That was it. "How'd you find out?" Jen asked, wiping her eyes.

"He called me and told me himself." Esther continued with difficulty. "He said, 'Aunt Esther, I have something I want to tell you. I want you to know this because I love you.' Then he said it. He said, 'I have AIDS.'" The phone line captured the audible cry that escaped from Esther.

"Oh my god." Jen held back the grief of many lost friends. "I hate this disease." She paused to compose herself then said, "You have no idea what he's gonna go through."

"I know it's awful," Esther, trying to pull herself together, said. "He sounded good though."

"So, is he actually sick? I mean, what symptoms has he had?"

"He had pneumonia and was in a hospital there in Lebanon for a week or so. You know what he said, Jen?" Esther's voice sounded contemplative.

"What?" Jen asked, breathing deeply.

"He said having AIDS was really helping him get his life in order. He said he'd been living his whole life in the closet and that was going to change. He wanted me to know he was gay. He wanted to get out of that small town and live somewhere he could be himself. He's been wanting to move to Seattle for a long time, so now he's finally going to do it."

"Really?" Jen dabbed her eyes with the sleeve of her worn denim shirt.

"He asked me to tell you all about it. He wanted to make sure I told you." Esther sounded responsible.

"I'll call him. Do you have his number?" Jen spoke to Steven only once. He was excited, motivated to take his life into his own hands, relieved to be open with Jen about his sexuality.

Steven did move to Seattle, immediately. After that, Esther visited him in Seattle a number of times before he died. Esther came to know Steven's partner, Cal, who had moved to Seattle with him, and cared for him until the end. She came to know Steven much better. Esther stayed with them in their apartment on Queen Anne Hill when she visited. It was clear to Esther that Cal and Steven loved each other deeply. She marveled at Cal's devotion and commitment. Steven got sicker, and Cal was right there for him.

"It's no different than how I cared for my husband when he was ill," she admitted to her friends over pinochle, after a long debate with herself about whether to bring it up. Esther noticed how the ladies glanced at one another, cleared their throats, and changed the subject. She didn't bring it up again after that.

Esther and Jen continued to speak on Sunday nights. Life seemed accelerated to Esther, and to Jen and Lisa, certainly to Steven and Cal. Esther kept Jen appraised of Steven's condition, which deteriorated rapidly.

Steven had gotten toxoplasmosis, a brain infection. It was severely debilitating, and fast. Esther treasured the time she had with him. She was awed by Steven's new openness. Steven told her about meeting Cal in a restaurant in Lebanon. How, after that, they'd run into each other in a bar in Portland, then started seeing each other. Steven told Esther that he and Cal never lived together for the four years they were involved while in Lebanon, because Steven was so afraid people would find out he was gay. He feared losing friends, clients, and colleagues. It was a small community, Steven said that was his excuse for staying in the closet.

Steven was very near the end when he told Esther he had feared losing her, too. A sharp pain literally shot through Esther's heart.

"You know, Aunt Esther," Steven said from the hospital bed in the apartment. He was very weak. "When I visited Jen in New York that time, she introduced me to Cindy — with such confidence — such pride. I couldn't even imagine it. And you know, I never even hinted — even to Jen — that I was gay."

"Well now, Steven," Esther's eyes ran with water as she stroked his forehead. "You've come a very long way, a very long way."

"I have, haven't I?" Tears rolled into his ears; he efforted a smile, a dying man purged of a lifetime of shame. He reached for Cal's hand, then reached for Esther's hand, and drifted into a coma. He never came back. Steven died three days later at the age of forty, just seven months after his diagnosis.

* * * * *

Lisa and Jen went to Seattle for the memorial service. It was April of 1991. There were very few relatives, most of whom Jen barely knew. But there were many of Steven and Cal's friends from Oregon, Spokane, and Seattle.

"Joe is coming, but Mya and Ralph won't be here," Esther said with obvious disappointment when Jen and Lisa arrived.

"Why not?" Jen asked, afraid to hear the answer.

"Well, they cannot condone Steven's lifestyle. They believe to come to his memorial would be to do so," Esther said, fixed on straightening napkins at the banquet table. "They didn't care to have to speak to his friends." Esther stared at the table as she spoke. "I told them that the day would come when they would regret that decision, and regret not comforting his partner. You know, Cal is a wonderful man." Esther stepped back from the table and punctuated her handiwork with an affirming nod. Jen looked at Esther as if she were seeing her for the first time. Her mother was old, and still growing. Lisa squeezed Jen's hand. Then Esther, with watery eyes, looked directly at them, "I'm so glad you girls are here." Then she hugged the two of them at once.

The memorial service was a party the likes of which only gay men can muster: smoked salmon, crab cakes, tapenadas, rustic breads, champagne, and an a cappella quartet from the Seattle Men's Chorus. Esther, though shy by nature, spoke readily with whoever struck up a conversation. She was anxious to learn how people knew Steven. Anxious to tell them she was his aunt. And very proud of him. Though she didn't have many, she brought all the pictures she had of him.

The trip was a whirlwind for Jen and Lisa. They barely got to see Joe and only had the chance to have breakfast with Cal the day following the memorial. After they returned to Manhattan, Jen and Lisa got a card from Esther. It was addressed to the two of them — for the first time ever. She wrote that she was tired out from the memorial service but so very glad that the two of them were able to make it, hoped things were going well, and she'd see them soon. Under happier circumstances. A postscript was added: she had decided it was time to get her own place again, apart from Mya and Ralph. She enclosed a newspaper article. The Seattle archbishop was put on probation by the church for his public support of gay rights. Jen put the press clipping on the refrigerator with a magnet along with the envelope addressed to the two of them.

More articles followed about the archbishop, who was ultimately removed from his responsibilities. "I just don't understand it," Esther said one Sunday night. "The guy is right. What right does the church have to condemn the love between any two people?"

"I agree," Jen said and silently hyperventilated at the New York end of the line.

A dialogue grew between them over the next year. The religious right began an antigay-rights campaign in Washington state. Esther was very tuned into it. "I don't know how these people can call themselves the Christian Right," Esther said one Sunday evening, "because they're *not* Christian. And, they're certainly *not* right." She sent articles monthly about right-wing conservatives protesting "special rights" for homosexuals. She sent an article about the Association of Churches supporting a state gay-rights amendment. She highlighted the paragraph stating the Catholic church had not yet joined in that support. Her note said, "Maybe it's time the Pope learn a lesson from some other spiritual leaders."

It was nine o'clock eastern time on New Year's Day of 1993 when Jen finally got through to Esther in Spokane. Lisa was asleep, curled up on the sofa, her head resting just next to Jen's lap.

"I've been trying to call you off and on all day," Jen told her.

"Oh, I know," Esther said catching her breath from hurrying to the phone. "Well, Mya had the traditional dinner at her place, and I was there longer than I thought I would be." Esther had moved into her own one-bedroom apartment shortly after Steven died. It was in a senior citizens' complex. Esther loved her independence. Swore she wouldn't give that up again if her life depended on it.

"So, how was New Year's?" Jen asked as she turned the volume down slightly on the Barbara Walters special.

"Oh, very nice," Esther said excitedly. "I fixed a couple of apple pies and took them over to the Poor Clares this morning. You know, they're not so cloistered anymore."

"They're not?" Jen asked and smiled, appreciating her mother's intrigue with those women.

"No, they've taken away the screens and the curtains," Esther said, still catching her breath.

"Really?"

"Yes, and I'm glad for them, you know. That would be an awfully hard way to live, so cloistered the way they were." Jen thought of the days when her mother was so enamored with that life. "Anyway," Esther said enthusiastically, "I wanted to tell you about the lunch I had yesterday,"

Jen settled in for another Mabel story, "Tell me."

"I had lunch with Barry and Winifred Brownstone."

"Really?" Barry had been Esther's boss for some twenty years. Jen had worked at the law office part-time in high school, so she was quite familiar with Barry and his wife, Winifred. Barry had retired before Esther. He and Winifred periodically took Esther out for lunch or dinner. "So did you have a nice time?" Jen asked with interest.

"Oh, yes, we had a nice visit. I really wanted to tell you about our conversation."

"Tell me," Jen urged, having no idea where Esther was going.

"Well, we talked about the firm and Marty Price and George Selmer, and pretty much caught up on everybody and everything. You know that Barry had been helping out at the Lutheran church they go to. Making furniture for the social hall."

"I didn't know he made furniture," Jen commented with dispassionate surprise.

"Oh, yes, he's very handy. Anyway, Winifred mentioned something about a couple at their church that they'd become friends with over the years."

"Yeah?" Jen's interest was waning, she was half listening to Esther and half watching Barbara question Tom Hanks.

"Anyway, I guess the Brownstones have done a lot of socializing with this couple. They play bridge together, even made a trip to Hawaii with them. So,

Barry and Winifred had been talking about that other couple for a bit, and Barry mentioned that the couple recently had a son die of AIDS."

"Oh, really?" Jen's full attention came back to Esther.

"And you know, when Barry said that, I noticed that he kind of shrugged or something. You know what I mean? He looked a little disgusted or something."

"Yeah?" Jen listened intently. Impulsively, she leaned across the oak coffee table and lit a small, white, holiday candle.

"So I said, 'What's the matter Barry?' And he said something like, well, he just didn't agree with that lifestyle. And I said, 'What lifestyle is that Barry?' And he looked at me, as if to say, You know what I'm talking about."

"So, what'd you say?" Jen was completely involved in her mother's story.

"Well, I didn't say anything. I just kept looking at him. And finally he said, 'Well, you know, the guy was gay.' And I said, 'Oh really?' "

"So what did he say?" Jen asked quickly.

"He didn't say anything for a minute. I just kept looking at him. Then he said it again. He said, 'You know what I mean, Esther, the guy was gay.' "

"What'd you say?" Jen muted the volume on the television.

"Well, I looked right at him and said, 'What's the matter, Barry, have you got a problem with that?' "

Jen switched the television off by remote. "You said that?" Jen was stunned.

"I did," Esther said calmly, with her signature resolve.

"What did he say? Did Winifred say anything?"

"Well, Win had gone to the bathroom at that point. If she'd been there she would have said something to get Barry off the hook. But she wasn't there so he had to speak for himself."

"So, Mom, what did he say?" Jen was dying to know.

"Oh, he said he didn't have a problem with that per se, but that it just wasn't right and he didn't know why anybody would choose that lifestyle." Esther repeated Barry's comments with cynicism in her voice.

Jen chuckled briefly at her mother's tone, then asked, "And what'd you say?"

"I said, 'Oh Barry, do you really think people choose to be gay?' I said, 'Do you think any one would choose to be hated and discriminated against?' "

Jen was genuinely awed by her mother. "So what did he say?"

"Well, he just sort of looked at me," Esther said nonchalantly.

"God, Mom," Jen exhaled as if she'd been holding her breath through the whole conversation.

"So, then I told him, 'Barry, you and I will never know just how much courage it takes to live in this world and be gay.' "

Pause.

Jen swallowed the lump in her throat. And swallowed it again. Finally, she spoke, "You said that to Barry?"

"I did," Esther said solemnly.

Pause.

Jen exhaled sharply a couple of times to regain enough emotional control to speak. The flame from the candle flickered, then flared briefly. Jen said quietly, "Mom, I just... that's incredible, all of it, everything you said to him."

"It was a nice visit," Esther said with satisfaction. "I've had a nice New Year's."

"So have I." Jen took a long, deep breath. She gazed at Lisa, sleeping, and said softly to Esther, "Mom, thank you. It's gonna be a really good year. Really good."

In the Way of Intimacy

It was three months after leaving the convent when Rome got picked up by a wildly sexy woman. Rome was in the poetry section of a leathery used bookstore in the University District. She was only half consciously scanning titles on the shelf when, directly in front of her, a teasing index finger touched the spine of a book entitled *Babel*.

"Have you read Patti Smith?" a voice behind her asked in an intimate library whisper.

Rome turned to take in the stranger . . . straight dark hair, lush olive skin, dark and dancing eyes.

Her lips were delicately chiseled. They reached naturally forward as if she were about to say *shhh*. Quietly dangerous, intensely tempting. Rome answered, "Actually, I'm not familiar with her."

A smile of intrigue slid across the inviting face. "Really? Well, welcome to the seventies." Her name was Sylvia, she was in town from Portland. She took Rome to an all-red apartment that belonged to a friend who'd gone to England. There were four windows in the walk-through, two at each end. All dripping with red drapery spilling into pools on the red-painted wood floors. It was above an Indian restaurant on University Avenue. Sylvia was crazy about Rome's name.

Changing names was, Rome believed, one useful thing she learned from the convent. She entered the sisterhood at the end of her freshman year in college as Rhonda: tall, blond, and boyish. She was ultimately more a survivor than a follower. Two years into it, she found herself with a mad crush on Sister Superior. Rome was awakened by the strength of her own sexual arousal, but not without consequences: desire, conflicted with guilt and shame. It even disturbed what had been dormant childhood memories of sex with Uncle Shep. Crisis. Way too much. She left the convent and christened herself Rome. Rebellion. The true signature of a recovering Catholic.

Sylvia and Rome made love for three days in curry-scented air. Sylvia made up scenes they acted out, and Rome got to make love while playing different personas. First, Sylvia cast Rome as a private eye and spun a sort of film-noir web throughout the room. Rome had seen enough Bogart pictures to play along with Sylvia's dream world.

Rome was sitting back with her heels up behind a big red desk when Sylvia began. "I'm looking for a good private eye," Sylvia said. Rome slid her feet off the desk, sat up in her chair, watched as Sylvia slowly walked around the big desk and stood next to her. Sylvia smiled seductively as she lowered herself into Rome's lap. "Unbutton my blouse," Sylvia told her. Rome followed directions down to the final stroke. And so it went, Rome's first experience making love to a woman was as a private dick.

They dozed only intermittently. They awoke to drink wine and eat hard rolls, cheddar cheese, blueberries, and begin again. They acted out all kinds of vignettes. Pretended to meet in a Parisian café. Posed as newly-assigned college roommates. Sylvia even concocted a scene as new friends on an Up-with-People tour. Sylvia always set the scene, and always cast Rome in control. Sylvia liked to be taken, made love to. She endowed Rome, sometimes step-by-step, but always amorously. Rome absolutely craved it, the power Sylvia gave her.

Late into the third night Sylvia started the scene that stayed with Rome most clearly all these years. Setting the stage, Sylvia narrated, like a past-life memory told in a shamanic trance. Rome fell silently through the facade of reality that thinly veils this world from all others.

They lay side by side, floating on a magic bed. Sylvia began with half-closed eyes. "We live in a very small village hundreds of years ago. We're young girls, still living with our families. We know each other, watch each other, secretly we love each other. We have never spoken of our feelings. My father discovered me with another young woman; naked, kissing, touching. A terrible sin, a scandal — he disowned me. I am publicly whipped. Humiliated. Tied naked to a cross." Sylvia stretched out across the bed. "Tie my arms." Rome obligingly tied each wrist to the bed frame with guilty scarves.

Sylvia went on, "I have been tied here for twenty-four hours, since last night. I've hung through the hot, dusty day. The townspeople scorn me. All day they persecute me."

Rome's eyes grew huge with anticipation. As Sylvia wove a story of penance, Rome spun back through her own universe of convent halls, sacristies, and chapels. Capriciously she relived her most favored and secret glimpse of Sister Superior. Hair uncovered, freely fallen. Her neck, calling to be kissed.

Sylvia whispered without so much as a glance at Rome, "I regret only that it was not you with whom I shared my love." Rome flushed...heated... captured. Seduced by a sacrilegious punishment.

"I hang, aching for your forgiveness." As Sylvia went on, Rome's every muscle swelled from the aphrodisiac...the power of absolution. Sylvia went further. "It grows very late. You slip away from your family. You come to me. You stretch a water-soaked rag to my lips. It awakens me. I suck it. Sin-filled, water drops roll down my body, praying to be wiped away, licked away. I hang, unable to touch you, unable to reach you. Able only to feel your breath."

The breath of power...the power of Rome. Sylvia was silent. The room, possessed. An unknown place...an unknown time. Rome slid to her knees. Ran her lips down the length of Sylvia, prone, bound, wanting. Rome knelt at the foot of the ceremonial bed of penance. She was wild with life. Burning...

her neck, back, legs, even her fingertips. Flaming. Her touch... fueled with passion.

"Please," Sylvia asked, her eyes pleading for forgiveness.

Rome's was the omnipotent touch of mercy. It rippled up Sylvia's legs with each caress, shivered through her breasts. Together, Rome and Sylvia were wild with liberation, unbound by convention, sacrilegiously ecstatic — an erotic crucifixion.

"Please," Sylvia longed for vindication.

Rome's exoneration began. Atonement trickled down inside Sylvia's thighs.

"Please," fervently Sylvia petitioned again, begging for it, loving redemption.

Lips of deliverance spread wide Sylvia's soul. Her cloistered scent of desire was volatile in the moonlit room. Stretched on a mythical cross, bound to be loved, Sylvia wept from the rhythm of Rome's pardoning tongue. In the night... on the verge... the very edge... yielding... submitting... surrendering. The throbbing dance of absolution. Forgiveness, finally... exploding! At last! At last... mercy... sweet mercy...

Mercy indeed. The magic bed landed safely. The shamanic trance lifted. Rome collapsed slowly into Sylvia, and Sylvia pulled Rome tightly to her.

The village became the apartment. Time began again, and they rested silently for a long while. Then suddenly Sylvia dropped all pretenses and role playing. She hugged Rome, told her she loved her and began to kiss her nipples, suck them, lick them. Until that moment, Sylvia hadn't actually touched Rome. Rome froze up instantly. An iceberg of anger. Disconnected from the glaciers of grief and rage issuing from her past: a debilitating legacy of incestuous sex. Rome couldn't stand it, being touched like that.

Momentarily, she wanted to strangle Sylvia with her bare hands. Instead, Rome lost absolutely all interest. She got dressed and walked out in the middle of the night without saying a single word, without so much as looking at Sylvia. Somehow, for Sylvia, such a wildly understated exit dramatically befit their intercourse. Sylvia was left breathless. Rome left cold and emerged in the darkness, distracting herself with harmless recollections of making out with a few boys in high school. Remembered Jerry somebody, a boyfriend for three months during college before joining the convent, a sloppy kisser. The affair with Sylvia was Rome's first real sexual experience, not including that Uncle Shep stuff when she was growing up. Rome was twenty-one when she encountered Sylvia. She and Sylvia haven't seen or spoken to each other since.

Sunday

It's a drowsy Sunday afternoon in the middle of May in the middle of Seattle as Rome stretches away the lonely sleep from her nap. It's all Rome can do to keep from constantly kissing her cat, Vita, on the lips. She kisses Vita's head and sits up in bed; Vita rides the wave. Rome reaches near the phone on the bedside table for the plastic bottle of spring water — American champagne. Takes a long swig. Vita bothers only to open her green eyes and gaze.

Rome has cautious hazel eyes and dark blond

hair. Layered in tangled waves, it's not too short, not too long. It falls loosely around her angular but soft face. She has that exquisitely handsome look that makes people unconsciously dreamy. She is tall: five-foot-ten, naturally on the slim side. She goes to the gym regularly and at thirty-nine is in good condition. By looks she could have been a model or an actor. But her forty hours a week as reference librarian feed her appetite for order, composure, and exacting knowledge. She has no children. Doesn't go to church anymore. And dutiful family visits are brief. Though she changed her name nearly twenty years ago, they still call her Rhonda.

Rome lingers with Sylvia in her thoughts and Vita purring near her belly. Rome makes no rush to dive back into this particular Sunday afternoon. Dinner plans later, but still time now to lounge. Rome is amazed at how often she thinks of Sylvia. And as she routinely does, Rome brings herself to climax remembering that scene — Sylvia tied to that imaginary cross. Vita hovers and purrs as Rome finishes her ritual.

Rome had always hated cats. She was raised to hate them. Her older brother tortured cats for sport. Her sister was terribly allergic to them, so as a little kid Rome learned that cats made people sick. But when Rome moved into her present house she discovered mice. She put down traps, did mice-be-gone spells, had fits. Rodent phobia. Finally, she resigned herself. Rather live with a cat than live with mice.

She found Vita at the animal shelter. Short, soft hair, muted gray, marbled with beige. A perfectly shaped little kitten head. White whiskers and a bushy chin. The moment Rome petted the sleeping beauty — oh, what an awakening... a mighty stretch. Rome picked her up and held her, and then the kitten caught Rome's eye! In exactly that instant, Rome fell into a love she imagined must be saved only for children. Rome kissed Vita on the top of her head over and over again, the bridge of her nose, her eyes, her neck, her paws, her belly. She so much wanted to kiss her little cat mouth, but didn't.

Rome brought the kitten home and named her after Vita Sackville-West. *Portrait of a Marriage* was a favorite book, hence, Vita, the perfect name.

Somehow, Vita takes the edge off the Sunday blues. Finally, Rome pulls herself out of bed. Pads into the kitchen, followed by the four-legged matriarch. The salad parade begins: red-leaf lettuce, yellow peppers, red peppers, mushrooms, and sunflower seeds. Oh, and tomatoes, for Jack. Rome smiles at Vita perched on the counter.

Rome met Jack the day she moved into her two-bedroom bungalow not far from the Ballard Locks. That was over five years ago. Jack came over to introduce herself and Rome thought Jack was a man. She has a bit of a mustache. Goes strictly by Jack. Wears men's work clothes every day of her life. Could pass much more easily as a man than a woman, any day. Women are shocked to find her in public bathrooms. Rome once heard a blue-haired lady ask her elderly companion coming out of a rest room, "Was that a man?" Jack ignores it — seemingly.

Rome has dinner prepared when Jack arrives. Jack goes to the refrigerator and opens a bottle of bubbly water, pours two glasses full. Their interaction is familiar and easy, free from sexual tensions and expectations. Nonetheless, Rome is ill prepared for what comes up this evening as the two sit down to eat salad and pasta out on the patio.

Jack is agitated, and that's odd. The air is absolutely quiet. It's weird, like all the crickets died. Rome glances around the red-brick patio. She looks at Jack. And Jack is crying.

"Jack, what's the matter?" It is strange but compelling to see her cry, like meeting an alien. Jack can't talk. Tears spill out. She begins to sob. "God, Jack, what's wrong?" Jack tries to say something. Chokes on the words. Breaks into deeper sobs. Rome moves beside her, puts her arm around her. "Come on, let's go inside."

Rome walks her in to the house. Only one table lamp lights the living room, casting a soothing soft light. They sit together on the soft, dark-green sofa. Rome swore the whole time she was growing up that she'd never own a green sofa like her mother always had. She keeps her arm around Jack...rocking...rocking...back and forth. Jack struggles to say something. Rome soothes her. "Just take your time."

Minutes pass by. Jack begins to calm down. She grows very still, with intermittent explosive little gasps, the kind that sometimes follow a big cry. Rome sits with her. The two women side-by-side.

"I'm pregnant," Jack announces.

Rome looks at Jack in absolute, undisguised shock.

"It's weird, I know," Jack says. "Imagine what it's like for me. A total mind-fuck."

"I don't get it." Rome is hanging in disbelief.

"Remember when I went to California for my cousin's wedding —"

"You had sex with a man?" Rome fires the question with no restraint.

"I got really drunk one night."

"So, what? You got drunk and had sex with... with a man?" Rome stares at her. Then looks away. Vita walks with dignity to Jack and sits at her feet. All three are suspended in a chain of silence for a few long moments. Jack stares at Rome's hands... Rome stares at Vita... Vita stares at Jack, solemnly.

"So, what are you going to do?" Rome asks, softly.

"I'm going to have it," Jack says with the resolve of one who's already made up her mind.

"You are?" Rome asks with another wave of disbelief.

"Yep." Jack looks out across the room. Rome, still absorbing the news, looks at Jack. Jack continues, "It's almost like a goddamn virgin birth. This kid is meant to be here."

Rome pauses, digesting. "Well... all right then... okay."

The baby is due in October, the same month Rome was born.

Monday

Rome has to be at Café Web this evening where the library sponsors a monthly internet poetry event. Poets around the world go on-line live. Various cafés worldwide participate with simultaneous live, on-site readings by actors.

At the Web, Rome greets people and seats them

at computer terminals. A benign task, until a not-small, truly handsome, dark-haired woman with striking, sapphire eyes walks in.
"I'm here for the poetry reading." Her lips are velvety smooth. Hair is black and thick, short and straight. It falls flirtingly forward, a threadlike waterfall into inviting pools. She wears loose, black, tuxedo trousers and a rayon shirt that matches the color of her riveting eyes. Long sleeves rolled to her elbows give way to relaxed forearms, strong hands with distinguished tailored fingers. Her neck... her face... every exposed inch of skin emanates something that gives Rome an appetite.
"You uh, you uh, you must be one of the actors?" Rome says, half tongue-tied.
"No, just an internet junkie," the stranger says attentively.
She can't be, Rome thinks. Not her. One of those people without a life? Up all night. On-line. In chat rooms filled with virtual geeks making virtual friends. Not with that skin. Not with that face. Not with those eyes.
"So, can I just sit anywhere?" The woman waits for Rome's direction.
"Uh, yeah. Well, uh, why don't you, uh, sit here, at this table. My table. I mean, there aren't enough terminals for everybody, so you have to share. So... you should just, you know, you should just sit here."
Oh, good, Rome, you idiot.
"My name is Lauren. And, I'm sorry, I didn't get your name?"
She's so articulate. "Oh, uh, Rome. My name is Rome."

"Rome. Great name." Lauren reaches out, shakes Rome's hand.

"Oh, well, thank you." Rome is dressed in a dark-blue linen suit, trousers and a blazer, with a short-sleeved white cotton shirt that got suddenly altogether far too hot. "Can I get you an iced latte or mocha or something?"

"An iced, double-tall mocha would be great. Here, let me give you some money."

"No, no, I'll get it."

"Are you sure?"

"Yeah, really. My pleasure." Okay, Rome thinks. Coffee, caffeine, sugar, and chocolate. All in common. This is good. She feels Lauren watch her walk over to the counter and talk to the orange-haired barista. "Lauren," Rome says to herself, liking that name. Lauren. She has a sexy sort of k.d. lang thing going, Rome thinks. Rome tries not to stare.

Rome manages to get back to Lauren without spilling, tripping, or dying. And then Rome begins. "Where were you born...where'd you go to college...what did you study...where do you work...where do you live?" They never even look at computer screens, or actors. Rome leaves everyone else on their own. She's enthralled with Lauren. When Lauren gets a chill, Rome takes off her blazer, puts it around Lauren's shoulders. Rome slides her right foot slightly between Lauren's legs and says, "Really? You're not involved with anybody?" *She's gorgeous. Available. My god. This is love. The fabric of life.*

The fact that Lauren starts sneezing is no deterrent whatsoever. Rome gets extra napkins for

Lauren to use at her leisure. Rome learns, after dragging it out of Lauren, that she is an astronomer, at the University of Washington. A cosmologist, to be exact. One who studies the structure and history of the universe as a whole. *Oh my god.*

"You took the bus here? Really?" Rome spots the chance to offer her a ride home, but doesn't want to move in too obviously. "So, you're a pretty serious environmentalist then?"

"I just don't have my car tonight because it's in the shop."

"Oh, I see," Rome still refraining from proposing a ride too quickly.

"But, uh, I do recycle," Lauren says quickly, not wanting to disappoint Rome. "And I shop at the food co-op." She scans her political-correctness resumé. "And I use a water-saver shower head," she says with commitment then retreats with an unintentional glance to the side realizing she sounds like a desperate job candidate groping for the right qualifications.

"Oh," Rome says, harmlessly enjoying a moment of clear control.

"I've got a rebuilt VW bug and I love it, but it's always in the shop. It's a bug. What can I say?" the astronomer surrenders entirely.

"So, can I give you a ride home?" Rome relishes the moment.

It's late as they walk to Rome's car. Rome looks up at the night sky. "So tell me about the universe, Lauren."

"What do you want to know about the universe, Rome?" Lauren asks, waiting for a cue.

"Well, I want to know about your favorite things."

"Hmmm, well, I agree with Rodgers and Hammerstein." Lauren softly sings the familiar tune, "Girls in white dresses with blue satin sashes..." She stops singing and simply speaks, "But of course one of my favorite things is Venus in the night sky."

"Venus?" Rome repeats with a plea in her voice to hear more.

"And there she is," Lauren points. Rome looks up, then at Lauren. "See?" Lauren continues, "She's usually the brightest planet."

"Hmmm, I see," Rome says dreamily, "and how about the brightest star?"

Looking directly at Rome, Lauren says, "The brightest star? Well now, that would be Sirius."

"*That* could be Sirius?" Rome said softly into Lauren's eyes. "Or *this* could be serious." Then, without a word, Rome slowly leans to Lauren and kisses her tenderly.

After a deliciously long, gentle kiss, Lauren resumes talking, though she looks at Rome. "The brightest star...is Sirius."

"Yes, it is," Rome says playfully with a charmingly serious look.

Lauren goes on looking at Rome. "It's about the same size as the sun." The two look right into each other's eyes. "But it gives off about thirty times as much light."

"Hmmm, I feel it," Rome says.

Lauren sneezes.

"Bless you," Rome says quickly.

"Thank you." Lauren pulls a tissue from her pocket.

"Pull your ear," Rome says, and reaches over and gently pulls on Lauren's left ear.

"Pull my ear?" Lauren smiles as she wipes her nose.

"It's good luck." Rome is charmed, even as Lauren sniffs and wipes.

Lauren sneezes again.

"Bless you."

"Thank you."

"Pull your ear." Rome pulls it for her again. "You have to pull your ear every time."

Lauren sneezes again.

"Bless you," Rome says again, and with each blessing moves closer to Lauren.

"Pull your ear," they say together and both tug lightly at Lauren's ear again.

"Come on," Rome says. "We better get you home."

Once in the car Lauren sneezes many more times than feels good and pulls her ears off. Her nose runs and runs. She blows and blows. Sounds a little like a ferry whistle, Rome thinks, endeared. More kissing would have to wait. The prelude could be enjoyed that much longer. When Rome drops Lauren at her house they exchange phone numbers between sneezes and ear pulls. Rome goes home alone and barely sleeps all night from the thrill of meeting Lauren.

Tuesday

Rome rides the escalator to the library's third floor the following morning, debating if she should call Lauren. She decides she'll hold off till after work. Then heads directly to her desk and dials. Restraint. Ha!

"So, how are you feeling?" Rome asks with consummate coolness.

"Much better." Lauren surmises, "It must have been an allergy attack."

"An allergy attack?" Rome says with concern.

"It's the only bad thing about spring. I just have to deal with it. I could hardly sleep last night. Thinking about you." Lauren purrs unconsciously.

"Hmmm, me too," Rome says, spacing out just a little.

"So, you wanna get together again?" Lauren asks.

Rome taps her computer keys mindlessly, distracted by a sudden yet familiar twinge of irritation at being blatantly pursued. "How about..." she realizes she hasn't thought this through at all. She has to say something. "Saturday" finally comes out.

"Saturday?" Lauren tries not to sound like she can't wait that long, but a little of that comes through.

"Yeah," Rome begins defending her terms. "It's the soonest I can..." Then shocks herself by finding Jack as a convenient excuse, "I've got plans with my neighbor and —"

"Listen, Saturday's great." Lauren recovers quickly.

"You sure?" Rome asks, giving Lauren a chance to plead.

"I can wait," says Lauren innocently, not needing control.

"Okay," says Rome, quietly tapping the space bar, biting the inside of her cheek. "Can you pick me up at the gym on Market Street at two o'clock?"

"It's a date." Lauren confirms.

Rome hangs up and lets out a big sigh. Relationships. Like fire and ice. She thanks her Uncle Shep for that, though she never dwells on it or him. Drops her head in her hand a moment. Wants to call Lauren back immediately. Finally, she dials. Not Lauren. She calls Jack. Leaves a voice-mail message. "We need to talk about the baby. Wanna go out for Thai food tonight? I'll be home by six."

That evening she and Jack walk to the restaurant. "How about Gus if it's a boy," says Rome. "I love that name."

"Gus? It sounds like pus." The conversation goes on till they walk back home and say good night. Rome never mentions a thing about Lauren.

Rome has dinner with Jack again the next night. Rome goes to the gym Thursday night. Works late at the library Friday night. And finally Saturday arrives.

Saturday

It's two o'clock Saturday afternoon as Lauren leans against the health club building, waiting in jeans with a slight split just above the knee. Thick-soled black shoes, a white T-shirt, a black leather jacket. Rome emerges from the gym, fresh and enthused, hurries directly over to Lauren as if she were pulled by an invisible line. Lauren watches Rome, still calmly leaning. Lauren reaches for Rome, takes hold of the front of Rome's jacket. Pulls Rome to her and kisses her lightly. Right there. In the middle of Market Street. In the middle of broad daylight.

Slowly, they let go of each other. Eyes open, finding the daylight somehow startling. Rome wonders if Lauren is always that aggressive. Rome is suddenly apprehensive, in spite of being turned on.

"Wanna get in the car?" Lauren asks quietly

Without saying anything more they both get into Lauren's car. The doors close tightly. Once inside they look at each other.

"Dig the bug," Rome says flatly about the car, thinking about what Lauren might do next.

Lauren nods in agreement with *whatever* Rome is thinking.

"We shouldn't jump into this," Rome says, putting her hand on Lauren's leg.

"No, we shouldn't. We won't." Again she pulls Rome to her and kisses her.

As their lips separate Rome regains control calmly, "Let's drive."

"Where to?"

"Just drive," Rome tells her firmly but quietly. Rome leans over, unzips the gym bag between her feet, and pulls out a bottle of water. Looking straight ahead she opens the container, puts it to her lips, takes a long and badly needed drink. She passes the bottle to Lauren and watches silently. "Turn in here," Rome says, and Lauren turns into a parking lot. Lauren finds an empty spot and parks. "Wanna walk?" Rome asks.

Out of the car, Lauren shyly extends her hand to Rome. This turns Rome on. She takes this sexy, dark-haired beauty's hand in hers and leads the way. She can't remember the last time she held a woman's hand in public. They walk together toward Lake Washington Ship Canal . . . down the wide sidewalk . . . past junipers that touch and hug each other. The smell of cut grass emanates from the manicured lawn. White crocuses and purple tulips dance in their beds. They stroll to the Ballard Locks. Three well-cared-for wooden fishing boats slowly rise from sea level to meet the lake. Water slaps at the huge concrete chamber. The two women watch. One fair, one dark. A pair of beauties. A picture of strength.

They walk across the skinny-railed, mitered gates at the end of the locks, and on to the railed walkway in front of the spillway dam. Sea lions luxuriate in the sun-splashed water. Rolling, gyrating, turning, performing for tourists who watch in dazed adoration. The two women walk to the fish ladder. Down the long concrete ramps. Down the twelve steps into a room under the water. A series of fish-viewing windows open into the underworld where the Pacific salmon run. Sleek and fearless fish, on fervently courageous journeys. Surreal, and startlingly intimate. Destined to spawn and die. Lauren and Rome together. Spellbound voyeurs. Watching as one power- ful, foot-long sockeye salmon flies from the left into the first window. It leaps to the next window. Suddenly it whips backward out of view. Gone. Two huge steelhead shoot into the first window. Together, a mighty pair. Each more than two feet long: strong and silvery; sleek and stalwart. Quickly they leap to the next window. And to the next. Tourists exclaim at the two, in awe, mesmerized — having only heard or read of the spectacle, never having experienced it.

Rome puts her arm around Lauren's waist. Lauren slides her hand up Rome's back. The salmon relentlessly pursue their mission. Driven by nature. Battling forces that all but hold them hostage. Finally, the two plunge in unison out of view from the last window into their destiny. Rome turns Lauren toward her and kisses her ... hot ... long ... and deep. Surrounded by tourists. A young girl bored with the fish is electrified. Her gawking mother tries to turn the girl's face away. The kid is glued. Other tourists try not to notice. Rome and Lauren let go of their kiss. Leave the fish to their fate. Arm in arm, they reemerge into the upper world.

Lauren drops Rome at her house. In the car they kiss goodnight. Rome's hands wander a little, and Lauren enjoys it. They do not, however, have sex.

Sunday Morning

The next morning Rome picks Lauren up on campus. Lauren likes to spend Sundays at the lab. It's quiet, just the way Lauren likes it best. They sit in Rome's car. First looking at each other. Then Rome touches Lauren's hand. Then Rome touches Lauren's leg. Then Rome's lips meet Lauren's lips ...

finally . . . delicately . . . very deliciously. Slowly, Lauren pulls away from Rome. To see her. Take her in. And just as Lauren is about to engage another kiss, she sneezes.

"Shit!" Lauren quips with frustration.

"Bless you," says Rome and pulls Lauren's ear without saying anything about it this time.

Lauren sneezes again. And again. And again.

"Shit." Lauren opens the car door and jumps out. She takes a deep breath.

"Are you okay?" Rome asks, leaning across the seat. Then she opens the glove box, yanks out a small package of tissues. "Here," handing them to Lauren. She gets out, runs around the car, and stands next to Lauren.

Lauren sneezes again. "You don't have a cat do you?" Lauren asks.

"You're not allergic to cats, are you?" Rome stifles her horror.

"I *am* allergic to cats."

"You can't be allergic to cats."

"I am though."

"You can't be. You just can't be."

"So you do have a cat?" Lauren says wiping and sniffing.

"Oh no, no, no, no, no. You don't understand. I don't just have a cat. I have Vita."

"Vita?"

"Vita isn't just my cat. I mean Vita's my . . . my . . . she's like my little soul mate."

"Soul mate?" Lauren asks with mild distaste.

"Well, you know, my *four-legged* soul mate." Rome quickly tries to make her animal bond more palatable.

53

Lauren says nothing, focuses on breathing.

Rome goes on, "My sister is allergic to cats, so I know it's awful. But this, this is horrible."

"There must be cat hair in your car."

"Cat hair." It is impossible for Rome to reduce any part of Vita down to a problem. "Well, there's cat hair everywhere in my life." Rome sinks into silence. *Gorgeous. Available. Allergic to cats. Cruelty. The fabric of life.*

Lauren blows her nose. The ferry whistle.

"I don't know what to do," Rome says earnestly.

"Let's do this," Lauren says, wiping. "I'll take the bus home today. And we'll just plan things so that we take my car ... and stuff."

"You'll never be able to hang out at my house," Rome laments.

"You'll have to hang out at my place then," Lauren says with moist, alluring eyes.

"Oh, I will, will I?" Rome says, half teasing, half disturbed at such a constraint.

"Yeah," Lauren tugs on Rome's shirt. Then sneezes.

"Bless you. Okay, I'll make sure I'm hair-free."

They both hesitate momentarily in their own worlds. Then Rome says, "Well, are you sure you don't want a ride? It's not very far. I mean, it'll only take a minute."

Lauren smiles regretfully. "I'll take the bus. It's not a problem."

Not a problem? That afternoon Rome cleans like a mad Cinderella. She does her car meticulously. Vacuuming. Scrubbing. Polishing. She does armloads of laundry: seat covers, throw rugs, clothes, sheets, and pillowcases. And she shampoos Vita. Whoa.

Monday

Exactly one week after they met, Rome readies for a date with Lauren. Though it is Monday night, neither has to work Tuesday morning. Rome makes sure her clothes are cat-hair free. She says good-bye to Vita, pets her head, then washes her hands. Vita looks at her: betrayed. Rome sees it in her eyes. She says her last good-bye of the evening, does her final hand wash, and into her car she climbs. Carefully. Onto a big plastic blanket that drapes over the front seat of the car. Uncomfortable, Rome thinks, this'll never work.

Rome arrives as scheduled at exactly seven. Lauren meets her at the door. Pulls Rome into her house, aggressively, Rome thinks. A telescope dominates the small living room. An impressionistic painting of some constellation Rome doesn't recognize hangs opposite the single front window. Oppressive, heavy fabric drapes the window. Rome wishes there were more windows. Or something. Avoiding eye contact with Lauren, Rome cruises the room... books ...science books... lots of books Rome has never heard of. Videos. A complete collection of Rodgers and Hammerstein musicals. Rome grins. Lauren walks slowly to Rome and kisses her. It's slow and deliberate. Lauren gets lost in it. Rome gets distracted. A chill comes over her.

"Hello? Something going on?" Lauren asks perceptively.

"Oh, I'm sorry, I just spaced out," Rome says trying to be casual, her breathing quickening, and eyes beginning to dart around the suffocating room. Panic: she's trapped. "I'm okay. Really." Rome tries to convince herself. Lauren looks at her lustfully: it triggers Uncle Shep stuff. A shiver races through Rome. She wishes they were at the Locks or a café or somewhere... just not here... trapped in this place.

Lauren lightly touches Rome's cheek, studies her. Rome simply cannot look her in the eye again. Lauren runs her hand softly down Rome's neck, to her shoulder. Another shiver shoots through Rome. She glances at Lauren, makes an effort to smile. Rome falls into the frigid, gaping chasm between them. Looks down at the floor. Then, Lauren tips Rome's chin up, and kisses her.

Rome stiffly pulls away, fighting off the inevitable anger.

"What's the matter?" Lauren asks, concerned, and unassumingly.

"Nothing." Rome grits her teeth, unconsciously. Her jaw tightens. *I'm fucked up,* Rome wants to say but doesn't. Instead, "Listen, I just can't do this."

"Do what?" Lauren asks calmly, looking for clues.

The house is jammed with Rome's old baggage... the uncle... touching... licking... sucking... penetrating... her good Catholic family... shame... all the stuff that lives between Rome and intimacy.

Lauren, unknowingly out on a limb, dares to comfort Rome with a loving touch. Rome's skin freezes. Lauren recoils, backs away. Rome's eyes skate across the wintry room, zero in on Lauren, freeze in a paralyzed silence. Rome struggles to reconnect. She squeezes her lips together, grabs at her own shirt, desperate to make contact with real time. "I'm sorry, okay. I'm sorry," she says. "I gotta go." Rome drifts slowly to the door.

Lauren, uncertain but moved, says, "Rome, tell me what you're feeling."

Lauren dares, cares to ask. Rome's eyes fly to her. A mob of memories gush to her throat. Her tongue swims hopelessly in her mouth. A plaguing numbness begins its familiar spread... stalks up her back... into her head. Tears leak from her shuttered eyes.

Lauren watches, a lifetime away. "It's okay, Rome."

"It's not okay." Rome manages, body gripped. "Look, I'm sorry." Looking away, a slight veneer smile intrudes on Rome's otherwise frozen face. Lauren watches Rome walk out, leave Lauren's house, her first and only visit. By the time Rome gets to her car at the curb, only the knowing might sense some ordeal has had its way with her. She has no benefit of catharsis, just a festering, unexpressed trauma. She remains as she was: an incested bomb awaiting its destiny.

Rome goes directly home and gets into bed. Vita joins her, sweet Vita, the object of Rome's affection. Vita rests in the middle of Rome's coping midlife chest. Rome holds her gently but tightly. Vita purrs... unconditional, unwavering, love.

The phone screams. Startles Rome. She answers in a hurry. "Hello?"

"Rome, this is Lauren. Are you okay?"

"Yeah, I'm fine." A long pause toys with the future. "Lauren, it's not gonna work." Fate sealed. "Please don't call me anymore." Rome hangs up. She begins to tremble... chokes back the burgeoning tumor of memories. Her right hand shoots into her hair and pulls. Tears fill the holes in her eyes. She curls up on her side, pulls Vita into her arms. She panics, her mind racing to think of something, something good. Jack... she thinks of Jack... and the new baby... the new baby... Rome catches her breath. She breathes. Then she hugs Vita and kisses her little cat eyes and her little cat head.

Bellevue Housewives

Bob's orgasm mounted inside Kate, and all she could think of was Susan.

The winter evening crept into the large bedroom like a stealthy spider, crawling down the walls and across the plush carpet, sneaking over the fancy baskets stuffed with fine bedding, descending on the dark green love seat near the cold fireplace. Kate was on her back. Eyes open, watching over Bob's shoulder. It fell on her.

"Oh god, I want you," Bob said, thumping on her, rhythmically. Turning her head sideways, she closed her eyes and imagined she saw Susan...only inches away...felt her breath. Kate rose up inside herself to hear Susan's whispers. Susan's liquidy lips moved. *What was she saying?* Longingly, Kate's hand reached across the bed, grabbed the sheet, and twisted it. In her mind's eye, Kate leaned as far as she could toward Susan, brushing Susan's whispering lips.

"Oh Jesus," Bob whispered. "Oh god."

Kate opened her eyes. Long-legged, insectlike hairs stood about the back of Bob's shoulders. Then, closing her eyes again, she searched inside herself for more images of Susan. And suddenly, Susan was on top of her. Their faces were secretly close together under Susan's long, silky, brown hair. Susan touched Kate's face lightly, kissing her. Softly at first; then harder. Kate ran her hands up Susan's back, like touching silk for the very first time. Then, Kate took hold of Susan and rolled her over. Susan acquiesced; Kate was on top. A cry slipped from Susan that had been seized inside. Forever maybe...she'd waited for this...wanted this.

"Oh god, oh god, oh gawwwd," Bob's final thrusts pushed Kate's fantasies of Susan out of the room. Kate became motionless on top of him, as Bob flattened like a leaky ball. "I love it when you get on top." He meant it; he loved it.

Leaning across him, Kate turned on the light. "Honey, I've got to get ready. People are going to be here any time." Dismounting, she stood. Then picked up the satin robe on the basket at the foot of the bed and wrapped it around herself.

Kate was striking: tall and sleek, shockingly blue eyes. Intense. A powerful presence, like a wolf. Streaks of silver laced through short, brown hair.

Fabric hung on her in a way that elevated clothes to an art form. She possessed that androgynous thing, very subtle makeup, tailored clothes. Men wanted her. Women wanted her.

Bob rolled his eyes. "Whatever happened to things like, Thank you baby, I've been dying for you?"

"Bawwb," she looked at him. "You came. I came. We've got a house full of people coming." She sighed, "I have to get ready." Then she turned away, walked into the bathroom, and closed the door.

He yelled after her with laughter in his voice, "Oh, come on baby, come back to bed."

Kate took a package of cigarettes from under a stack of towels, opened the window, leaned against the wall, lit up like an old pro. She looked across the lot to the neighbor's house. Desire.

Susan. They'd just met in front of a moving van only days ago. It was a gray December afternoon. Kate returned home in her Benz from the Bellevue Country Club. Parked. Watched her a few minutes. Susan had a clipboard in hand. Milled about with the movers like they were old friends. Wore shorts, a polar fleece jacket and earmuffs. That silky hair, very light brown, almost blond. Athletic like a dancer, not tall. Kate walked toward her. Took off her shades.

"Welcome to the neighborhood." Kate approached with a smile.

Susan switched her focus from the movers to her visitor. "Thanks." She took off her earmuffs.

"I'm Kate Chase. I live next door."

"Susan Mendles, nice to meet you."

They shook hands. The sounds of movers fell distant. The overcast sky suddenly was charged with energy. A flock of snow geese glided effortlessly over them. They looked up. The old black lab whined from the yard next door. They looked over. A dashing tuxedo cat scampered up. Laced his body between the two women. They leaned down and petted him. He purred.

"Well, Buster..." Kate stroked the length of him, looked at Susan and said, "This is unusual. He doesn't normally take to strangers at all."

"Really?" Susan looked at Kate, smiled. "Hello, Buster. You sure are handsome." She petted him intently. Their hands innocently touched as they fondled him. Unexpectedly, a metal hand truck crashed to the street. Buster ran off. The two women stood up.

"So, is there anything you need? Anything I can do?" Kate asked.

"You know what, I really need to make some phone calls, and I left my cell phone at the hotel."

Kate situated Susan at the table in her kitchen. Susan began her calls. Kate poured two glasses of wine, one for Susan, one for herself. Then Kate went about unloading the dishwasher as Susan used the phone. Soon, Kate poured seconds for them. Kate watered the plants placed all through the five-thousand-square-foot house. She returned to the kitchen, poured thirds for the two of them, sat down at the table, and watched Susan. Susan finished a call, clicked off the phone, sipped and smiled.

"Okay, let's see," Kate said. "You're about thirty-two, from California. Husband's in the computer business. You're a lawyer. You exercise occasionally, eat whatever you want, and never gain weight."

"Not quite," said Susan. "I'm thirty-four. From Wisconsin via California. My husband is in international trade. I own a dating service in L.A. Plan to open one here. I'm an aerobics junkie. Strict vegetarian. Caffeine free. Sugar free. Except, I drink alcohol without restriction." Susan laughed. She leaned her head down on her outstretched arm and looked up at Kate. Kate took a last swallow from her glass. Delight spread across Kate's face. "What?" Susan asked dreamily. A savored moment. Then Susan snapped to, "I should go check on the movers."

Kate dismissed that idea. "They're professionals."

The doorbell rang. It was a muscled guy from the moving gang. They were done. Susan and Kate strolled through Susan's new house. Checked things out. Susan signed off. The guys left. Susan collapsed on a sofa. "I gotta get something to eat." She looked at Kate and said affectionately, "Wanna have dinner with me?"

Kate thought out loud, "Let's see, this is Wednesday. Erica doesn't get home 'il eleven. Jason's skiing. I'll leave a note for Bob. Okay, let's go."

As they walked out the door Susan asked, "Who's Erica?"

The restaurant was designed for privacy. Plants created secluded settings. Lighting was soft and confidential. Candles flickered intimately on tables. A waiter placed two martinis in front of them.

"I don't usually drink so much," Susan said, relaxed.

"This is an occasion." Kate raised her glass. "Welcome to Bellevue."

Susan raised her glass. "I think I'll like it here. I don't know if my husband will," she laughed, "but I will."

They drank. Salads came. They ate. Talked. Laughed. Sighed. Entrées came. Ate some more. Talked some more.

"Okay, let me review," Susan said. "You're from here. You have two, almost-grown kids. You're about... thirty-nine."

"... about thirty-nine," Kate laughed.

"And your marriage is..." Susan looked questioningly.

"... a problem," Kate admitted.

"A problem," Susan repeated carefully. "You've spent the entire afternoon with me. And the entire evening. And will you be taking me to my hotel?" Susan looked her in the eye.

In the car at the hotel Susan asked Kate to come in.

"Not tonight," Kate responded.

"Okay then." Susan leaned over and kissed Kate at the corner of her mouth. Stopped within inches and said, "Thanks for everything today." Then she kissed her on the lips.

A piercing telephone ring in the bedroom brought Kate abruptly back to the moment. She shot a look at the bathroom door.

"I'll get it," Bob yelled and snapped up the handset. He threw himself back on the pillows and answered. "Hello?"

He heard crying.

"Thank god, it's you, Bob," a woman's voice whimpered.

Kate opened the bathroom door and looked at

him. "Is it Jason?" Kate asked, referring to their nineteen-year-old son.

He covered the receiver with one hand. "It's Sheila from the office."

"Where the hell is Jason? I have to talk to him," Kate said.

"He's off with some friend somewhere." Bob waited for Kate to leave him alone.

She closed the door again. Leaned against the counter. Took a long drag. Released. Tossed the cigarette in the toilet and turned on the shower.

Bob watched the bathroom door. "Okay, okay Sheila, calm down. What's the matter?"

"It's Mickey," she said faintly, talking about her husband.

"Mickey? What about Mickey?" Bob was desperate to know.

"I told him I'm leaving him —" she broke off.

"You didn't tell him about us did you?" He sat up fast on the edge of the bed.

"Well, no, not yet," she cried more.

"Sheila, Sheila, Sheila. Sounds like you need to blow your nose, Sheila." She blew. "You have to just take it easy. You hear what I'm saying? Where are you?"

"I'm at the mall."

"The mall. Good." He got up and paced, his tall, wiry, hairy body taut with extra tension. His dark eyes looked darker; his tight curly black hair undisturbed. "Okay, Sheila. Sheila, listen to me. This is very important. Whether you leave him or not, it's very important that you do not tell him you've been messing around."

"I haven't been messing around. I love you Bob. I can't wait to see you tonight."

"You're still coming?"

"Yeah," Sheila sniffed. "Mickey doesn't want anyone to think anything is wrong. I didn't argue. I'm dying to see you."

"Okay, okay, so look, you'll come here tonight. But Sheila, you've got to be very careful about this."

"Bob, I love you."

The shower stopped.

"Yeah, listen, I gotta go. I'll see ya tonight." He switched off the phone. Collapsed on the bed against the pillows.

Kate stepped into the room wearing her robe. "What'd she want?"

"Directions." He got up, headed to the bathroom.

Kate picked up a pair of earrings. Could see Bob in the mirror. "Directions were in the invitation." She said it matter-of-factly.

"She lost her invitation," Bob said in a distracted tone and closed the bathroom door. The shower spurted.

Kate dabbed perfume on her neck...massaged lotion into her hands, up her arms. Photographs arranged on the nearby cherry bureau summoned her...memories. She picked up their wedding picture. Twenty years ago.

They'd met at college and gotten married during their last undergraduate year. Kate and Bob Chase. Kate never finished college. She was three months pregnant with Jason who was now in his first year of college at Cal Arts. Creative. He was home on break. Erica had just turned eighteen, going on thirty-five. Brainy. Already applied to Cornell, MIT, and a few other places, planning to be a research scientist in genetic engineering. Kate and Bob had lived most of their married life in Medina, a very well-off section of Bellevue, the city situated across the east side of Lake Washington from Seattle.

Bob emerged from the bath. Preoccupied, he dressed quietly and quickly. Kate returned to her vanity and put on a light layer of mascara. Bob was an architectural engineer, president of his firm. He had designed the fifty story Northwest Bank Building in Seattle, and the Media Communications building — others too, in Portland, Minneapolis, St. Louis. His family was nouveau riche, having only known success. He picked up his shoes, kissed Kate on her neck, walked out of the room, and closed the door.

She suddenly remembered opening the front door that day last summer when she'd come home unexpectedly. Supposed to have been at a workshop with her friend Eva, but the instructor was sick. Bob and the kids thought she was taking a cooking class. Actually, it was supposed to be a past-life workshop. She and Eva did things like that. No one else knew.

"Let's do facials," Eva had said. "And enemas."

"I'm not in the mood for an enema," Kate said. "You can, baby. I'll go get the stuff. It's in the cabinets downstairs in the laundry room. I'll be right back."

She went down the carpeted basement steps. Approached the laundry door. Heard voices. Familiar voices in unfamiliar tones. She stopped. Listened. The sounds were odd. Unidentifiable, yet not uncommon. Intrigued, she opened the door slowly.

It took a minute for them to notice her. Jason. Naked... on his back... on the old oak table. His legs were propped up on the shoulders of his friend Brett, who was also nude. Brett's penis was in Jason's ass. Jason pinched his own nipple with one hand, and with the other, he masturbated.

Kate watched until Jason noticed her. He saw her and screamed, "Get the fuck out of here!"

She said flatly, "I hope to hell you're using a condom," then closed the door.

"Come in, come on in." Kate ushered in Norman, Bob's business partner, and Norman's wife, Diane. The Chase's holiday party had begun. They hugged, kissed on cheeks, presented bottles.

Norman stood straight like a penguin, wing-tipped heels unconsciously touched. "Right on time." He smiled hugely in a way that made his strange little round face seem independent of his large fleshy head.

"Well, Norman buddy — and his lovely bride Diane Helman," Bob said too loudly, already a bit liquored. "Or is it Diane McKenna? I'm tellin' you, Norman, all our wives are gonna start using their maiden names, and we can thank Hillary for that."

Norman hooked his thumbs in his front pockets, rocked back on his heels and laughed. Diane rolled her eyes. Kate liked Diane a lot, though they had very little interaction. They had known each other for years. But Diane was agoraphobic. Intensely reclusive. Sadly beautiful, like an alien. Her showing at the party was her semiannual outing. Everyone accepted her rare appearances as normal.

Kate proceeded to take their coats when Tristan, the houseboy she'd hired for the evening, interrupted. "Mrs. Chase, allow me," he reminded her with consummate attentiveness, and took the coats. Then covertly he said to Kate, "You just enjoy yourself, dear, I have it all under control." Something about his tidiness reminded her of Jason.

Through the glass entryway Kate saw a car pull into the circular drive. Jeff and Nia Morris. Jeff got out of his BMW wearing his suit and trademark bow tie. They were followed in by Jeff's partner, Harold Easton, from one of the original northwest timber families. Jeff romanced Harold into financing a direct broadcast satellite business. That brought Jeff and Nia out from New York.

Nia had that glossy, magazine-cover look. Her skin was flawless, the color of black tea with a splash of milk. She was a tall, skinny, native New Yorker with wild, black hair; rich, dark eyes; and flirty lips. Nia reveled in leisure. Loved to read magazines, get massages, luxuriate in baths, see movies, float in pools, cruise the lake, shop, drink coffee in cafés, talk forever. And she lived for affairs.

Nia and Kate started at a dinner party for Nia and Jeff after they moved to Bellevue. It was Kate and Bob, Norman and Diane, Jeff and Nia, Harold, and two other couples. Nia was a quiet, sizzling star. Effortlessly, she gave off energy. Made everyone she spoke to feel important. She focused unobviously, but intently, on Kate. Fell crazily, surreptitiously in love. The rest of the party didn't have a clue. Except of course, Kate. They sat next to each other at the table. Nia was smooth as satin. She complimented Kate's Valentino suit, her Chanel No. 5, her Picasso earrings, and her Italian shoes. Asked about her hair.

Who did it? Her sign. What was it? Kids. Did she have any? Fun. What'd she do for? Marriage. How long? Bob. Was he good? Women. Had she ever?

Had she. Indeed. Nia and Kate were lovers for nearly a year. Friends ever since.

In the entryway, Nia leaned against Kate's cheek, whispered in her ear. "Hmmm, hi sweetie, where's my Eva?"

Kate smiled beyond Nia. "Right behind you."

Nia turned around. Looked at Eva, her designated center of her universe. They embraced amidst the party arrivals. Quite a couple. Only Kate was the wiser.

Eva was a five-foot-six-inch beauty. Choppy, wavy, reddish-brown hair. Juicy brown eyes layered with facade and mystery. A hesitant mouth. Mature, enticing breasts that made everyone weak kneed. Flat stomach. Toned arms. Incredible legs, slim and well shaped. Worked out daily. Intensely present in her body.

Eva was Kate's best friend. They'd met in college, forever ago. They were lovers, off and on, for years. Years. Eva had finally divorced her husband to be with Kate. Kate couldn't do it. She just couldn't leave the security of her marriage. Eva and Kate had ended their affair two years ago. Eva never really got over Kate.

Eva hugged Kate. "Susan coming?" Eva asked.

"So to speak," Kate said looking outside. Eva and Nia turned to look, no attempt at subtlety. "Yoo-hoo," Kate sang to redirect their attention. "She said she'd be a little late."

"Shall we leave you to your guests?" Eva inquired.

"I guess," Kate quietly lamented.

Eva proposed to Nia, "Come into the kitchen with me, will you?" Nia slid her arm through Eva's. "You may want to join us, dear," Eva said to Kate. They strolled away, furtively together.

Kate watched them, then followed, spotting Jason along the way. "I tried to track you down all afternoon," she said to him discreetly.

"I don't know if I want to know," Jason looked in the direction of his dad.

"Well, you do want to know. You're negative," she pushed her lips together to keep herself together.

Jason closed his eyes. Breathed. Opening his eyes, said, "Thank you, Mom, for getting the results for me. I just couldn't... I uh..." He kissed her. Kate's watery eyes shut, and she clutched his shoulder. He said, clearing his throat, "I didn't mean to spoil your party."

Kate asked with interest, "You staying?"

"For a while anyway." Jason watched guests arriving. "I can't pass up a party."

"Jason, where's Erica?" Kate asked, dabbing her eyes with a cocktail napkin.

"She hates these parties you guys throw." He sipped his drink. "She's probably hiding under the basement stairs."

Kate kissed him on the cheek. "Sweetie, would you greet our guests for me?"

He smiled handsomely. Well-groomed, fit, charming. "Hmmm, happy to. There are benefits to having a homosexual son, you know. I love to entertain." He swept away.

Kate caught up with Eva and Nia in the kitchen and sat on a stool at the counter with a relieved smile. Eva poured Kate a drink and set it in front of her. The kitchen was big, with a huge stainless-steel refrigerator and freezer, tons of cupboards, an eat-in bar, and the informal dining table where Kate and Susan had gotten half drunk.

"Susan wants me to go to the San Juan's with her for a couple of days." Kate smiled. Eva and Nia looked at her, then each other, and back at Kate.

"When?" they asked in unison.

"Tomorrow," said Kate.

"What about her husband?" Nia asked coolly.

"He'll be away on business for five days."

"A reason to be cheerful, no?" Eva raised her glass with mixed emotions.

"No, I'm just kidding," Kate cajoled.

"What?" asked Eva. Relief slipped across her.

"Susan hasn't asked me to go anywhere with her," Kate clarified. "Hell, I just met her."

"Oh, fuck you!" Nia exclaimed and threw a hand towel at her.

"How long has it been?" Eva asked, trying to control her curiosity.

"What, since we met?" Kate asked for clarification.

"Yeah, since you met," Eva acted nonchalant.

"Barely a week. I haven't even seen her since that first day."

"You haven't?" Nia turned up her nose.

Eva didn't hold back, "You live right next door. How could you not see each other?"

"I don't know."

"Different schedules?" Nia supposed more to herself than anyone else.

"But we've talked on the phone," Kate added.

"Phone sex?" Nia asked quickly.

"No, we didn't have phone sex, for God's sake, Nia," Kate said surprisingly prudishly.

"Oh, it's not like you've never had phone sex," Nia said accusingly.

"You two had phone sex?" Eva asked. She sort of pointed at Kate and said, "How come we never had phone sex?" Then to Nia, "And excuse me, but I don't recall any digital woo-woo with you either."

Nia picked up a celery stick and chomped on it. "Tonight's the night, honey," she said to Kate.

"What? For phone sex?" Kate asked just to be a smart ass.

"No, no, smarty pants, you won't need a phone tonight," Nia said knowingly.

A short, nervous, dark-haired woman burst in the kitchen, followed by Tristan.

"Sheila!" Kate said, recognizing the woman. "Something wrong?"

Tristan began arranging a tray of hors d'oeuvres, not missing a beat.

Sheila went directly up to Kate. Stood stiffly, speaking with a conscious effort to move only her lips, no other facial muscles. "Kate, I'm sorry, but this is an emergency."

"What is it?" Kate asked.

"Have you got a tampon?" Sheila asked in a pinchy whisper.

"Oh, yeah, in the bathroom closet. There're thousands. Help yourself," Kate offered.

"Thank you. Thank you *so* much." Sheila dropped her puffy eyes. Then looked up. Scattered her eyes across the three women and Tristan. Then quickly. "I'll just excuse myself then." She turned to exit.

"Oh, Sheila," Kate called after her. Sheila stopped and looked at her. "They're recycled. I hope that's okay for you," Kate said with a straight face.

"Recycled?" Tristan loudly dropped a silver tray, stifling an outburst.

"Yuck," Sheila backed away with suburban disgust.

"I'm just trying to do my part," Kate said modestly.

Sheila looked at each woman, then Tristan, mouth half opened in an *ick* position. Then she bolted out the swinging door.

"Recherché!" Tristan applauded with his voice. With trays in tow, he pushed the door open and left.

Referring to Sheila, Kate said, "She's fucking Bawwb." Kate smiled at Eva and Nia. "But then, so am I."

"You are?" both Eva and Nia exclaimed.

Eva went on, "What's up with that?"

Then the swinging door produced Susan, catching Kate by surprise.

"Hi," Susan said, looking at Kate. "That Tristan said you might be in here."

"She's here all right," Nia said getting up. "You must be Susan. I'm Nia."

"Hello." Susan was incredibly becoming. Very short, black dress, black stockings and heels. She looked at Eva. Eva sized her up as mannerly as possible.

"This is Eva," Kate finally jumped in, looking at Eva with a little frustration.

"Eva, nice to meet you," Susan said politely. She handed a package to Kate. "I brought some pâté and a bottle of Scotch."

"Thank you," Kate took the goods.

"Ah, Susan," Eva said with intent to embarrass, "I think you've got some mud or crap or something on your shoe."

"Oh, no, really?" Susan looked apologetically at Kate. "I'm sorry." She spotted paper towels and wiped at her shoe.

"We'll leave you two be," Eva said. Then to Nia, "Sweetie, let's go see who's here, shall we? Bah-bye, Susan." Eva guided Nia out with her.

Kate didn't look at Susan right away, swallowing the rest of her drink, pouring another, head down. Slowly, she looked at Susan. Susan poured herself a drink and sat next to her at the bar. They drank in silence.

Finally, Kate started to say, "Susan —"

Just as Susan started to say, "Kate —"

Both laughed nervously. And drank.

Susan started again, "Kate, I can't have an affair with you."

"You already are having an affair with me," Kate said, soothing Susan with soft eyes.

Susan studied Kate's face, "Am I?"

Kate slowly nodded an affirmation, kissed her with her eyes. "You are."

Susan's hand fell away from her glass and slid over to Kate's, touched her. "I suppose I am."

The door swung open. Susan pulled her hand away. It was Eva.

"Is Nia in here?" she pretended to look around as if she'd just lost her. Eva was checking up on Kate.

Kate and Susan shook their heads slightly.

Eva split.

Kate and Susan looked at each other with desire.

Susan put her leg between Kate's, on the rung of the stool. "I had this all planned. I was gonna come in and tell you I couldn't, you know, see you like this."

"And..." Kate waited.

"And then I see you like this and..."

"And..." Kate waited.

Susan kissed Kate lightly on the lips.

The door flew open again. It was Jason. He stopped abruptly. They both looked at him. "I'm sorry," he said. "Excuse me, please. I was just looking for Tristan." He backed out. "I didn't mean to interrupt." The door swung closed. The women looked at each other. The door burst open again. "Dental dam," Jason said with a soft voice and exaggerated lip movements. Again, he disappeared.

"Oh, Jesus," Kate said and dropped her head in her hand.

Susan stood up. "God, I'm sorry. I'm gonna leave. I've gotta leave."

"Come on," Kate implored. "Don't be sorry, and please don't go."

Susan attentively brushed Kate's hair away from her eyes. Then boldly but calmly, Susan asked, "Go away with me will you, just for a day?"

"What?" Kate was pleasantly flabbergasted.

"Go somewhere with me," Susan said with pleading eyes. "Just for a day. So we can spend some time together. Just the two of us. We can talk, and just be together. Alone."

"Okay." Kate sort of collected herself and tried to think straight. "When?"

"Tomorrow. Meet me at the ferry terminal downtown at noon," Susan said with urgency in her voice.

"Noon?" Kate tried to clear her head.

"Is that too early?" Susan asked with an almost businesslike tone.

"No, no. Noon is fine. Okay, I'll meet you at noon." Kate stood up, a bit bleary.

"I'll see you then." Susan hesitated as if she were about to kiss Kate again. Then, she disappeared in a flash.

Kate's liquor crashed in on her. She walked to the freezer. Opening the door and leaning into it, the frosty air surrounded her face. She took an automatically-made ice cube from its container and placed it on her forehead, her cheek, her neck. She opened and closed her eyes a few times. Put the ice to her lips. Then she pulled herself together and went to join the party.

She moved through the formal dining room and into the living room. It was like walking into an Andy Warhol exhibit. Bob was momentarily captured in a pop culture scene, frozen, and duplicated a dozen times. His image reappeared in every room. Next to him, his benign partner Norman. And Diane, tragically beautiful. There. There was Eva. Oh god, Eva — captured tenfold — vibrant and sexy. Over and over again — Nia — provocative. Image after image.

Kate wafted through the gallery of people. Half of whom she'd slept with. Some mother, she judged herself. It was as if she were wearing headphones and hearing only her own breathing. She found a wall, steadied herself. Rubbed her temples gently. She saw Eva again. Nia had her hand on Eva's leg. Kate laughed to herself. So much happened right in front of everyone, and no one ever noticed. Maybe no one wanted to notice. Except Jason, of course. Wait a minute, Kate was saying to herself. Something seemed wrong — between Eva and Nia. What? Eva moved Nia's hand off her. Were they fighting or what? Nia walked away and left Eva sitting there. Kate would find out everything later, she thought to herself, leaning against a wall and closing her eyes briefly

Then Kate scanned the exhibition again, watching, editorializing display after display. Harold dripped dip on his tie. Norman and Bob flipped through compact disks. Bob yelled out titles loudly to no one listening. Norman moved about Bob doing some geeky dance. Poor Norman: Norman Nobody. Then there was Tristan: debonair, fetching. Taking care of everything. Jason: talking with Tristan. Oh. Jason and Tristan. Of course. Sheila: hair-sprayed bangs, drinking by herself in the wing chair in the corner, watching Bob and crying. Mickey: icky Mickey. No wonder Sheila didn't want him. He balanced a beer bottle on his face, performing for other women from Bob's office. Diane: agoraphobic and still here. A miracle, Kate thought. Kate wished she could drag herself over to talk with Diane. Such an opportunity. Wait. Nia — Nia was approaching Diane. Interesting — how Diane looked at Nia. Hmmm... Nia and Diane. Nia and Diane? Who would have thought, Kate wondered? Eva. Where's Eva? Kate drifted through the spectacle. Have you seen Eva, she asked? Excuse me, have you seen Eva?

Kate's phone rang the next morning. It was Eva. "Swell party," Eva said without much emotion.

Kate fell back in the bed, checking for Bob. Not there. "Where were you? I looked for you."

"I left. I just needed to leave. So what happened with Susan?" Eva seemed all business.

"I'm supposed to meet her at the ferry terminal at noon. Will you take me?" Kate asked, with a genuine need in her voice that was pleasant to Eva.

"Noon?" Eva questioned, buoyant at being needed by Kate. "You better get in gear darlin', it's already after ten. I'll pick you up in an hour."

They parked under the Alaskan Way viaduct, across the avenue in clear view of the waterfront.

"We made it," Eva said with surprise in her voice and turned off the engine.

Kate perused the landing from the car. "I don't see her." Both women silently scanned the waterfront. "My life is so fucked up," Kate said rather casually.

"Oh, don't start," Eva responded without even glancing at her.

"Well, it is," Kate said, like a teenager mumbling under her breath.

"Everybody's life is fucked up," Eva said without apparent sympathy. "You're not so unique you know."

"I hate that," Kate curled her lip.

"What?" Eva asked nonchalantly.

"That you're-not-so-unique crap."

"Well, it's the truth," Eva chuckled.

"Oh, yeah, like you're some expert in the truth," Kate patronized.

"Actually, the truth is," Eva pondered a second, "I think your life is fucked up."

"Oh, well, thank you very much," Kate chuckled at Eva's boldness, glad at her directness.

"Well, you said it first," Eva gladly pointed out.

Pause.

"I mean what *are* you doing with Bob?" Eva blurted.

"I don't know," Kate said with amused defense. "Bob's actually a good guy." They both snorted. "I just bring out the worst in him. We bring out the worst in each other. The only thing Bob and I did well together was Jason and Erica."

"And what's up with you and this Susan?"

"Nothing's up. We just met. She's attractive. She's fucked up. I like her. What can I say?"

"Ya know what," Eva said, "I'm just gonna say this and you can do whatever you want with it." Eva was bolstering her courage.

"Well, don't hold back now, bumpkins."

"You're so goddamn smart Kate, and you aren't doing anything with yourself."

"Uh, excuse me," Kate responded with attitude, "I'm raising two kids."

"Your kids are raised, Kate. My kids are raised. All our kids are raised."

Kate shot back, "Okay, okay, miss know-it-all, seer-of-all-things, oh sage-of-life, soothsayer. What exactly do you suppose I might be able to do with my self?"

"I don't know," Eva thought quickly. "Go into real estate."

"Oh, fuck you." Kate pushed Eva's shoulder and laughed.

"What? Some of my best friends sell real estate," Eva said seriously, but with a grin.

"There she is," Kate exclaimed, spotting Susan. Kate opened her car door and said, "Let's go."

"I'm not going with you," Eva was quick to clarify.

"No, I mean, just walk over there with me, will you please?" Kate implored.

"Look, I'll just wait here till you leave," Eva said insecurely.

"No, Eva, go over there with me, please?" Kate asked fervently, focusing on Eva until she relented.

"Oh god, okay. Why? Why do I have to go with you?"

Kate hurried to Susan who was looking out over Elliot Bay.

"Susan," Kate went right up to her.

Susan looked at her, tears in her eyes.

"What's the matter?" Kate asked slightly out of breath.

Susan turned away from Kate and out again to the water. Eva caught up to Kate, stood next to her, and looked across the Bay. The three women at the waterfront. The ferry whistle blew.

"I'm sorry, Kate," Susan said through tears and began to back away. "Forgive me, but I can't do this," she said slowly, then turned and walked away.

Kate watched Susan go. Then Kate turned and stared over the water, standing next to Eva.

Finally Eva said, "Wow. She *is* fucked up."

Kate smiled. The remark brought her out of

herself. They both gazed at the glassy water, silent for a bit.

Finally Eva asked rather matter-of-factly, "Do you remember Debbie Wildmon?"

"Debbie Wildmon," Kate repeated thoughtfully. "From college?"

"Right," Eva said. "She owns a big bakery on Bainbridge Island." Eva glanced sideways at Kate, hoping to see her reaction but not wanting to make an issue out of looking at her.

"Debbie Wildmon," Kate said again, still thinking. "You mean the one we all thought was a lesbian?"

"She's got a big house on the water there," Eva continued looking forward. "I can practically see it from here."

Kate looked at Eva and asked, "How do you know where she lives?"

"I've been there many times, Katy," Eva smiled widely, still not looking at Kate.

"Evaaa. Come on, we have to stop with these secrets." Kate bumped Eva's shoulder as she spoke and looked at her.

Eva continued to scan the Bay when she said, "I ended it with Nia."

Kate watched Eva to see how she was. "I had a feeling something was going on last night."

"Yeah," Eva finally glanced at Kate.

"How come?" Kate asked.

"It just wasn't working," was all Eva offered.

The seagulls filled the air with squeals in the quiet moment that passed between them.

Kate summoned up a sincere, "Too bad."

"Yeah, well, it's not like I was in love with her,"

Eva said without hesitation and without looking at Kate.

Another moment of quiet passed between them, the two sets of eyes exploring distant shores.

Finally Kate said, still gazing across the bay, "Yeah, well, you know what? I'm still crazy as hell about you, Eva."

Eva laughed.

"I am, goddammit," Kate protested, looking at her seriously.

"Yeah, you're crazy about me, you're crazy about Suuusan, hell, you're just plain crazy, Kate."

"I am not," Kate objected.

"You are too," Eva held her ground.

They both stared at the bay.

A tender smile flowed from Kate, and she said, "Hey, I've already admitted I'm screwed up, but that doesn't change the fact that I'm wild about you."

Eva looked at Kate, then took up with the bay again. Kate put her arm around Eva.

"So this, Debbie . . ." Kate began slowly, ". . . you think she'd want some company?"

"Probably," Eva said, nodding, a smile hinting at the corners of her mouth.

"Think she'd want a couple of roommates?" Kate asked with a chuckle, looking at Eva.

"Maybe," Eva said, attempting to hold back a big, wide grin.

The ferry whistle blew again, and the two women headed for the boat, arm in arm.

Before Dawn

The newly reelected governor was a sexy guy, even to a lesbian. Jo was relieved the victory celebration dinner party was wrapping up. She couldn't stand the social obligations connected with her job, but she was very adept at them.

"It's unbelievable. He's probably slept with half the women in this room," quipped Judy Fricht in her usual pursed-lip way. Her red paint had worn off, and her lips were peeling. She was a once-beautiful woman aged in bitterness and liquor, now unattractive by any measure. "And I don't mind telling you I'm not among the half he's had."

"Hmmm," Jo licked her lips softly, unconsciously compensating for Judy's dry mouth. There was a story behind Judy's selection for the governor's cabinet. Rumor was that the governor and Judy dated in high school. Judy had gotten pregnant, was sent off to have the baby, and gave it up. She started college a year late and the Honorable Foster Chandler had been trying to make it up to her ever since.

Jo scanned the room without a trace of effort, pained as she was to be there. She noted every fine detail of the evening's ending. Her teasing eyes were in constant alert; her flirting mouth could say everything without uttering a word.

Judy babbled on about the pangs of infidelities. "I don't know how or why his wife tolerates him."

Jo's eyes finally found Colleen Sawyer, across the white linen-covered tables, standing in an open doorway, stooping to talk with a couple of men. Colleen, a lawyer, was the governor's liaison for lesbian and gay affairs. An amusing title, Jo thought. Within seconds, Colleen spotted Jo and smiled slyly across the room of unsuspecting, intoxicated bureaucrats. Colleen was the most out person Jo had ever known. She could see Colleen's pink triangle lapel pin on her tux, along with the curled and crossed red ribbon... an AIDS activist too, of course. Jo knew the silence of their affair was killing Colleen.

"Tell me, Jo, which half are you among? Those he's had, or those he hasn't?" Judy asked stiffly, attempting to conjure conviviality in her voice. She barely turned to face Jo.

Jo's eyes rolled over Judy slowly and deliberately, like a street paver. "Judy, our man won, and we're in office for at least four more years. Congratulations," Jo raised her empty champagne glass toward Judy. She then said, with ambiguity, "I suppose, under the circumstances, knowing what makes Foster Chandler come isn't such a bad thing, is it, Judy?" Jo carefully punctuated her last comment with a choreographed stream of exhaled smoke. Smoking was a cover, a facade that helped cloud her uneasiness and nervousness.

Jo glanced Colleen's way but couldn't find her now. That was it, Jo had had enough. Her neck was flushed in a painfully familiar way. She hoped she hadn't turned red in the face, as she had a habit of doing when colleagues probed her personal life. She put out her cigarette, dropped her gold-plated cigarette case into her pocketbook, and clasped it shut.

"I'm jealous at how guiltlessly you smoke," Judy remarked, not sure if Jo had been insulting her.

"Smoking doesn't cause guilt; thinking about it does. Just don't think about it, Judy." And with that, Jo headed for the door.

The head of transportation, John Sherman, the state boys club, managed to snag Jo as she was leaving. "You won't reconsider Lopez Island this weekend, Joanne?"

"Thank you, John, but I can't." Jo searched the room for Colleen with no luck.

"It's always the same with you, Joanne. I used to think it was just me, but I haven't seen anybody else get any further with you since you've been out here."

"Get any further with me?" Jo shook her head,

smiling. She put her hand on his arm and said, "I'm flattered, but I can't this weekend." Then she walked away casually covering her annoyance, lightly smoothing the lapels of her dark blue blazer. She cleared her throat and waved good-bye to the gang across the banquet room.

Driving home Jo ran her hands through her hair and glanced at herself in the rearview mirror. The longer hair was working for her. It somehow raised less suspicion, she believed. The cold November air was calming; her hands relaxed on the cool steering wheel. The elections were over. Her job was secure, she thought. Foster Chandler liked Jo a lot. That was clear from the moment she met him at a Clinton fundraiser a year earlier. She had gone to his hotel room that night in Ohio, where she was living at the time.

"You're so enigmatic, Joanne," Foster had said with his back to her as he stood at the mirror fastening his belt. "You should be in the Northwest, land of Twin Peaks. You'd fit right in." He recruited her for a cabinet level position in Washington state at the age of thirty-eight. Not bad for a closet case from Marietta.

She turned the corner onto Plain View Road and pressed the garage door opener. There sat Colleen's Jeep. She stopped the door before it opened all the way and pressed it closed again. She should never have given Colleen that transmitter. But if she hadn't, Colleen would park right out front for the whole world to see. Jo parked on the street and headed quietly to the front door, checking to see if any neighbors watched. It was unlocked. Colleen always did that when she got to Jo's first. Why couldn't she leave it locked? Jo wondered. "I'd like to unlock my own door, thank you very much," Jo muttered under her breath.

She walked in tentatively. Murphy greeted her. He was a talkative cat, always happy to see her. "Hi, Murph, got company huh?" Jo surveyed the living room. Nothing out of place. The lines on the carpet from the vacuum still perfect. No sign of Colleen downstairs. She stopped to check the answering machine on the kitchen counter.

"Hello, honey, it's your mother. Just calling to see how you're doing, if you've been out with that John fellow yet, the transportation man? Well, love you. Call me later." The crease in Jo's forehead deepened as she closed her eyes. It was a way of keeping her mother's hope alive, telling her about the invitations she got from men.

Climbing upstairs, she saw light flickering on the walls in the bedroom. There was Colleen, in the candle lit master bath, waiting. The Jacuzzi steamed. Jo walked in slowly, leaned against the counter, and looked at Colleen. She began to unfasten her cuff links.

"Come here," Colleen said sitting up, making room in the swirling tub.

"I thought about you all day." Tension lived in Jo's face. "Did anybody see you?" she asked.

"I don't think so. It was dark." Colleen tried to lighten things, "Don't worry, my car was disguised as a man." Colleen climbed out, stepped on the thick white rug, and unbuttoned Jo's blouse. She reached up Jo's back and undid her bra. Jo's skirt fell to the floor as Colleen unzipped it. Jo stepped out of her dark blue heels, and Colleen bent to kiss her waist as she removed Jo's stockings and panties. Jo's head fell back slightly, her eyes closed. She inhaled deeply and slowly. Colleen pushed Jo's blouse and bra off her shoulders and gathered Jo in her arms. She buried her face in Colleen's warm, wet neck. Then pulling Colleen's face to hers, opened her lips to let Colleen in. The whirlpool was one of their favorite places. They'd had many a date there. In fact, most of their dates were at home.

They'd met at the winter festival in a local park right after the first of the year, shortly after Jo had moved there. The festival was an annual event to draw people back downtown after the holiday frenzy had quieted. There were musicians, dancers, steaming drinks, and hot food.

Jo had noticed Colleen in the crowd as a performance began at the park's gazebolike stage. Jo had gone uncharacteristically out of her way to stand next to her. Colleen was one striking woman with wavy red hair and beautiful bronze skin. She was forty-two and very self-assured. At five-feet-ten-and-a-half inches tall, she was noticeable under any circumstance. Her stature combined with her confidence gave her an incredibly compelling presence.

Jo spoke first. "Excuse me," she said as someone conveniently shoved her into Colleen. "I'm sorry." They locked on each other. A door flew open within Jo. She said, enthusiastically, "I'm Joanne Holden, I don't believe we've ever met." Applause from spectators around seemed to be for her.

It was as if Colleen had been waiting for her. "You seem very familiar to me, but I don't recall meeting before. I'm Colleen Sawyer."

Jo's heart pounded and her body radiated in the

cold, festive air. The bare sycamore branches surrounding the small park laced together, protecting the moment. The ritual drumming and rhythmic dancers on stage captured the age-old moment of spellbinding love. Jo stood perfectly still next to Colleen, hot from head to toe, watching the dance. Colleen moved closer and stood slightly behind Jo, then leaned ever so lightly against her. It was indiscernible at the crowded event. And for one fleetingly liberated moment, Jo leaned back against Colleen, in broad daylight, against this woman, this perfect stranger.

Jo pushed the door open even further, not wanting to lose her. She said, "Are you doing anything after this?"

"Well, I was hoping to have a date..." Jo drooped slightly when Colleen spoke, "...with a woman named Joanne I met downtown today."

Jo didn't hide her embarrassed thrill.

That night it started, the two of them... together. Jo trembled at Colleen's first touch. Tears filled her eyes; she was unable to contain her emotions. The night dissolved into a myriad of loving nights. Each time Colleen reached inside her, a door would open up within Jo and out would come another secret from her soul. Memories cascaded in tears, visions erupted in laughter, dreams appeared in sweet embraces, fantasies ignited in desperate frenzies. Jo was wide open with Colleen. "We have to go somewhere, where we can be together, live together." Jo could barely believe what slipped from her mouth, yet did nothing to retrieve it. She meant it.

"We don't have to go away to be together," Colleen said calmly but with resolve. "Jo, I can't live that way."

Jo craved the place she found in Colleen's arms: safe, warm, away from the rest of the world. It was a place where she was free to fall into her own depths and have someone there to catch her. Jo wanted someone who could save her from the conformity she demanded of herself when the alarm went off each morning, a conformity that allowed no room for this, this sort of thing she had with Colleen. "There's no place for it. If I brought you to my agency Christmas party, my career would be over. Times aren't changing. Not for women who've worked as hard as I have to get where I am. There's no room for it."

"I've made a career of being out," Colleen said. "I mean, look at me. The problem isn't with the rest of the world, Jo, the problem's with you."

"If I was going to come out, I should have done it a long time ago. And if I had, I wouldn't be where I am now."

"Come on, Jo. I don't understand," Colleen said patiently.

"People despise queers." Then Jo admitted, "Look, I can barely tolerate half the gay people I see."

"And where does that leave me?" Colleen asked.

"I love you," Jo pronounced softly.

"And I'm a woman."

Jo responded, "So, I just happened to fall in love with another woman."

"For the second time," Colleen was quick to add. Jo had told her way too much.

Jo said no more. She slid under the comforter on the feather mattress. The whirlpool had sent Jo in so many different directions. She was relieved to have landed safely in Colleen's arms. Colleen stroked Jo's hair and said, "It doesn't have to be this hard, baby." Colleen's words wrapped around her like a warm cotton blanket, as Jo drifted off to sleep.

She didn't even stir when Colleen left that morning. Before dawn. That was their deal. But normally, Jo would wake up with Colleen for a bit and then go back to sleep. Jo went downstairs to brew some decaf. Murphy trailed behind. On the counter she found a note from Colleen.

Dear Jo, I'm going to make this easier for you because it's too painful for both of us this way. I want the whole world to know how I love and care for you. I thought as time passed, you'd become more comfortable, not less. Being the light of your life only behind a closed door is not want I want. I can't go on hiding away with you. Please know that I love you. Colleen.

Colleen's garage door opener was left on the counter by the note. Jo picked it up and clutched it close to her heart. The thing fell from her hand. She braced herself on the edge of the counter. A frightening burst erupted from her chest. Choked her. She ran water, splashed her face. She quickly reached for the phone, accidentally leaning on the answering machine. Her mother's message replayed.

"Hello, honey, it's your mother. Just calling to see how you're doing, if you've been out with that John fellow yet, the transportation man? Well, love you. Call me later."

Murphy nudged her. She placed the phone back on the receiver, staring at the answering machine. Then she walked stiffly out of the kitchen to the hall closet where she kept the cat food. Glancing at the front door, she noticed it was unlocked. Colleen never had a key. Jo opened the door slightly, looked out at the neighborhood. She wondered if anyone had seen Colleen leave early that morning. Then slowly, she closed the door and locked it tight.

Meeting Magdalene

The last thing on Sarah's mind as she left Washington National Airport was love. It was a late Tuesday afternoon in May of '94. She was scheduled to arrive in the Northwest at eight P.M. She gained an extra three hours of work time traveling west, firing up her laptop computer the moment the 757 was airborne. She wiped the small matrix screen clean and placed the special lint-free cloth neatly in its plastic case, which went back into the side pocket of her Armani suit jacket. Sarah was handsomely put together: slim, tall, and effortlessly cool; surprisingly disheveled, short brown hair; attractive; brown, searching eyes. She was evaluating a project plan for an enormous computer system being developed for the state of Washington. The last time Sarah was in Seattle she was too young to remember. The Seattle World's Fair, 1962. She had been only three.

She took a cab to the Rainier Plaza Hotel on Highway 99 next to Pam's Park and Fly across from SeaTac International Airport. She removed the gray Calvin suit from her carryon and hung it up along with its companion off-white linen blouse. She plugged in her modem at nine-fifteen P.M., read through twenty-three new electronic mail messages, answered the seventeen that required responses, and shot off a note to her assistant to schedule lunch at the Noodle House on Dupont Circle for Friday's meeting with new clients — the Psychic Institute based in Norfolk. She hadn't even stopped to think what a departure they would be from her typical bureaucratic fare. She was asleep by one A.M.

Sarah was pressed and prepared by seven A.M. Wednesday for her trip to the state capital, Olympia. A state employee picked her up twelve minutes late. Sarah blew through the necessary meetings with automatic ease, but bowed out of business lunches to meet an old college friend who'd settled in Olympia. Jean. A wild-ass blond who majored in love affairs at Georgetown. Their one attempt at sex together was during their junior year. The climax came with a pizza delivery: they made better friends than lovers. Instead of sleeping together, they picked up girls together. Liked the same type... voluptuous, dark, sexy, smart, and daring.

Jean pulled up to the intersection of Capitol Way and Union in an old blue Toyota pickup and double parked. Smiling big time, she jumped out of the truck. All five-feet-ten-inches of her. Narrow-hipped and broad-shouldered, she wore close-fitting black jeans and a long-sleeved, blue-denim shirt. Her eyebrows arched in soft attention over happy blue eyes. Her blond layered hair resembled the shag cuts of the 1970s.

"God, it's been so long," Jean said with a smile as broad as her shoulders. She threw her arms around Sarah. "I am so fuckin' glad to see you!" Squeezed her tight.

Sarah wheezed, but gave in to the hug.

Jean pulled back, holding Sarah by both shoulders and looked her in the eye. "You still have that goddamn asthma?"

"Kinda," Sarah said through half a smile. Pulled out her pocket respirator and gave herself a quick blow. "I can't believe you ended up in Seattle."

"This isn't Seattle darlin', this is Olympia," Jean offered with swaggering charm.

"That's even scarier," Sarah said as she glanced at the old gas station across the street that had been converted into a drive-through espresso bar. A big, plywood sandwich board sat out front with a steaming coffee cup painted on it along with the words JO TO GO.

"You aren't gonna know what livin' is till you get outta that fuckin' city, Sarah. This all you brought?" Jean asked, picking up a black synthetic garment bag appointed with various zippers and buckles.

"Just that and my computer," Sarah said. Her

laptop bag was slung over her shoulder. They headed to the back end of the canopied truck and deposited the bags.

Sarah looked at Jean closely when they got in the truck and said, "I feel like I just saw you yesterday."

"It's that karmic family thing." Jean had a way of saying things in rolls and waves. Everything ushered smoothly from her. She appeared perpetually at ease, massaged by the act of living.

They ate at a little Japanese place on Main Street. Miso soup. Salads. Sashimi. Attempted to fill in blanks between holiday cards of the last fifteen years... Sarah's career journal... Jean's spiritual adventure... numerous names of the various women who'd shaped their lives. Magdalene was prominent on Jean's list of the last year.

"I can't believe you have to leave today," Jean said as she grabbed the bill away from Sarah and dug cash from her pocket. "Can't you stay through tonight?" She laid a stack of bills on the table, and they meandered outside.

"No, I really need to get home," Sarah said, casting her eyes over the faux waterfall positioned among a bevy of statues and birdbaths for sale across the street from the restaurant.

"I can't believe," Jean said as they climbed into the truck, "I have to take that lie detector test today. I mean, I absolutely have to do it. There's no way I can reschedule it."

"You really want to be a cop that bad?" Sarah watched closely for her reaction.

"Come on, can't you just see me?" Jean said cajoling.

"I would be scared shitless," Sarah said without

apology. "Come on, what's the attraction, really? The uniform? The gun?"

"The handcuffs," Jean said without missing a beat. "You're sure this is okay with you? I feel kinda weird droppin' you off like this."

"Really Jean, it's fine. Come on, you're doin' me the favor. I'll just work while I'm waiting for you. I've got a lot to do. Oh god, listen." Sarah turned the radio up. "What's this remind you of?" It was an old David Bowie song, "Changes."

Jean snorted. "Oh my god, the Triangle Club!" They both cracked up. Sang every word together, too loud, off-key, laughing.

Jean parked the truck in the dirt driveway along side the house. "Okay, so you'll wait here a couple of hours, then I'll come back, pick you up, and we'll head to the airport."

"Okay," Sarah said. "It's an hour or so to the airport, right? That'll give us more time to talk."

"Yeah. And you'll get to meet Magdalene," Jean said as her cheeks lifted into a smile. She got out and went quickly to the back end of the truck, pulled one of the bags out, and approached Sarah just as she emerged.

"Here Sar. Sorry, there's some dirt on it. This is the computer bag, right?'

"That's it, thanks," Sarah took the bag, wiped at the bottom of it, and placed the strap over her shoulder. She then fixated momentarily, trying to shake the dirt from her fingers.

Jean pulled a skeleton key out of her pocket. "Here, take my house key. I'm not sure she's home yet." She dropped it into Sarah's cupped hands. "Use the door around on the front of the house. That key doesn't work in the kitchen door. I gotta go, or I'll have to lie about being late." Jean bolted around the front end of the truck, and Sarah followed her. Jean stopped suddenly before opening her door, turned around, grabbed Sarah, and hugged her tightly.

"You better go, princess," Sarah said like a taunting sister.

Jean pulled back with her nose wrinkled. "I can't believe you called me that. You can't ever do that around here," she glanced about. "You understand? I mean it, Sarah."

"I'm glad we got to have lunch," Sarah said with a quick sigh, feeling pressured about the time.

"Me, too. God, I love you."

Sarah opened Jean's door to hurry her on, and Jean jumped in. Sarah slammed the door and waved, "Bye-bye, princess!"

Jean started the engine, pressed her face against the window, and mashed her nose to twice its width. The tires spat dirt as she drove away.

Sarah stood alone on the dirt drive. It got very quiet as she watched Jean drive away. The small, inviting house waited behind her. She just stood there, smart and handsome, in dirt, daylight, and bounding organic matter. She was suited expensively, buttoned up, with her electronic connection to anywhere hanging under her arm. Finally, she turned to face the house. Dogs barked distantly. A fence with an arbor over the gate separated her from the place. To her left, a tall laurel hedge grew at the end of the short driveway. It ran proudly between the house and the road a hundred yards or more. She hesitated briefly, then with conjured urban suave placed her hand on the wood gate before her.

It had no latch. She pushed the wide thing open almost as if she were carefully walking it. It creaked comfortably, sounded like the amused groan of an old know-it-all. It punctuated her entrance with the solid sound of wood against wood as she closed it. Her eyebrow went up. She lifted her hand from the wooden character, brushed her fingers together, and flicked her hand slightly as if to shake off the encounter. She turned. To her left the laurel hedge held court. To her right the little house sat, looking much bigger, fully adorned with flowering baskets hanging gracefully and happy blooms jumping out of the ground in every direction. She felt the old gate and its friendly fence behind her, guarding the suspiciously animated environment.

She dared a step. A raven cried. She stopped, glancing about, tightening her grip on the shoulder strap, tugging at her collar unconsciously. An urbanite. Rurally challenged. She could, with savvy, handle major international airports, concrete mountains, chaotic cities, and mass humanity. But dump her on to dirt in the middle of trees, bushes, and country air and watch her squirm like a worm. This is ridiculous, she thought, forcing herself to proceed. She was slow, casual, and thoughtfully cool. Through the blossoming eyes of a thousand plants, she proceeded. Several steps along on the red-brick walk, she felt her foot unintentionally land in something. She stopped, lifted her shoe to see the bottom, expecting to see dog doo or something. She realized instead that she'd stepped off the brick and onto some mossy grass. She looked up at the house in front of her. Annoyed. She continued around the corner of the house. The walkway changed from brick to concrete — a comfort zone, but it narrowed. Huge rhododendrons jumped out from both sides, made the passage even narrower. She turned sidewise and scooted through the blossoms without touching the massive things.

She'd arrived at the front porch, which was missing its steps. She grabbed hold of a paint-peeled post. Pulling herself up, she hit her head unavoidably on a fuchsia that hung with spirited insistence. Finally, she stood tall on the front porch. Paused. Surveyed the parklike yard that spread before her. Two cedars soared straight into the sky just in front of her. A chestnut stood farther back. A willow draped the area to the left. Under it rose a large birdbath, poetically concrete, held up at the base by a striking trinity of naked women in dancelike positions. They were long, slender, and powerfully present. They reigned over the purple wild flowers, green ground cover, and everything else nearby. One with arms stretched out low to her sides. Another with arms resting above her head. The third, a mystery unseen from Sarah's perspective.

Sarah readjusted the shoulder strap as she turned toward the door. With key in hand she aimed for the lock and discovered the door was already slightly open. A lace curtain draped the window in the door. She couldn't see, so she knocked and slowly pushed it open.

"Hello," she said softly and scanned the small room. No one was there. She waited a moment. Then again, "Hello?" She stepped about halfway in. "Magdalene?"

No answer. She entered. Two large windows were flocked with off-white veiling. Dead ahead was a small, altarlike table. At the center was a strange stuffed creature with a long body about ten inches high. No arms. No legs. All body. Yellow with black polka dots and a proportionately right-sized, black head with great red straw hair that stuck straight out like a fan. Unlit candles flocked the thing on all sides. On the wall above, a huge scarf was draped like a snake. About it hung a variety of stuffed dolls and a crucifix. To the right hung a large wall sculpture. Four pairs of animals, posed nose to nose, cut out of metal, surrounded by a windowlike, arch-shaped metal frame. Four metal cups held four votive candles on each side and four down the center, one at each conjoined nose. Beyond was the entrance of what looked to be the kitchen.

The room was dominated by a long, tall, skinny bedlike structure draped with blankets. A couple of pillows puffed at the far end. To her left just inside the door was a low-built piano topped with beads, shells, a metal dancing woman, and two framed photos, both of Jean, holding closely a shorter, dark-haired woman. Sarah moved forward into the room stepping onto an elaborate oriental rug. A couple of steps into the small room she stopped to look through a hall to her left. A door was open to a bedroom where the afternoon sunlight spilled onto a handsomely clothed double bed. Black fabric draped loosely from the ceiling above it.

Sarah veered right around the narrow bed,

heading toward the kitchen. She walked closer and closer to a large hanging photograph framed in a pale-pink feather boa. It was of a beautiful, naked woman stretched back gracefully into the arms of three dark women in long black dresses. They all looked right at Sarah as she approached. She watched them over her shoulder as she walked from the room.

Sarah stepped into the kitchen, turning. And there she was. Magdalene. Eyes closed. Seated at a round dark wooden table, she was listening to a Walkman through a headset. She moved her head ever so slightly to some rhythm. A candle and incense burned on the table in front of her. Her hair was shoulder length and the color of mahogany, lips moist, well defined, and painted several shades lighter, a strong straight nose, and high cheekbones. Eyelashes spread out like stars from her closed lids. Her rich olive skin was soft and luscious. She wore a cotton T-shirt with a torn neckline, and resting on seductively ample breasts was a handmade necklace, of two smooth, oval stones fused together with leather and a metal eyelet. Her body was full, substantial, yet small framed.

Sarah started to say something, but stopped and continued watching. Her computer bag slid slightly off her right shoulder. She lowered herself into a chair at the table, Magdalene seated just to her left. Only a brick structural pillar imposed a side of itself partially between them. Sarah studied her as if looking at a painting. Magdalene's hands rested in her lap, hidden from Sarah's view. Magdalene licked her lips. Sarah's eyes widened. Magdalene took a deep breath. Exhaled.

Suddenly, Magdalene opened her eyes, blinked

once, and looked directly at Sarah. Her eyes were wide and dark brown and moist with life. A wave of tentative excitement swept across Magdalene's face. She quickly took off the headset. Her hair fell loosely around her face. "Sarah?"

Sarah, not holding back her smile, rose from the chair somewhat nervously. "I knocked and called your name, but I guess you didn't hear me."

Magdalene watched as Sarah, standing somewhat awkwardly, pulled the strap snugly onto her shoulder. Then leaning forward, Magdalene blew out the candle. Sitting back in her chair, she took Sarah in. "That's a very sharp suit you have on there, Sarah."

"Oh, thanks, it's old, 1991. Got it at Davincci's in Georgetown," Sarah said automatically.

"You were watching me," Magdalene candidly commented, surprising Sarah.

Sarah smiled at the assertion while Magdalene watched her. "Just briefly. I mean, I didn't want to disturb you," said Sarah, ending her defense with a reserved eye-to-eye contact.

Magdalene held Sarah in her gaze and finally said, "I've been expecting you." Then she broke her focus. "Tea?" She got up from the table and walked across the kitchen to the stove.

Sarah followed her with her eyes. "No, thank you. I don't drink tea."

"Oh, you don't?" Magdalene said conversationally as she looked toward Sarah and filled the tea kettle.

"I thought coffee was the drug of choice in the Northwest." Sarah noted Magdalene's lack of conformity.

Magdalene tossed off a smile, placed the kettle on the burner, and turned the heat up. "I'm sorry to say I don't even have any coffee in the house." She leaned back against the counter, smiling at Sarah.

Still standing, Sarah said, "I'm fine, really."

A sudden knock at the kitchen door startled Sarah. Without waiting for a response, the door swung open with familiarity. In walked a woman of about fifty, wearing a gray business skirt and jacket and a black blouse, clutching in one hand a worn leather briefcase. Her hair somehow added to her sense of urgency with its dark roots and spiky white ends. She burst in and closed the door hard behind her before she realized anyone else was there with Magdalene.

"Oh," she said with utter surprise. "I'm sorry. I didn't know you had company." She stood stiffly in front of the door, placed one hand over her stomach, and glanced sideways at Sarah suspiciously.

"Don't worry, come on in," Magdalene said reassuringly from across the room.

"No, really, I can come back later," the woman said nervously, waving her hand just hip high in Magdalene's direction. "No problem."

Magdalene hurried over to her, "Ellen, relax." Then she emphasized, "It's not a problem." Sarah crossed toward the door as well, arriving in front of Ellen the same moment as Magdalene who casually tossed off introductions. "Sarah, Ellen. Ellen, Sarah."

Ellen, annoyed, quickly scoped Sarah out from head to toe and back up again.

Sarah extended her hand. "Nice to meet you, Ellen."

Ellen shook her hand, looking down at Sarah's feet and up again, "Nice shoes."

All three sets of eyes fell to the floor. Sarah let

go of Ellen's hand and said automatically, "Eighth Street, 1993."

All three looked up and at each other. An odd moment of silence landed on the triangle. Ellen glanced at Magdalene with irritation and impatience. Sarah was slow to pick up the cue. Finally, Sarah said earnestly to Magdalene, starting for the living room, "Uh, I'd be happy to wait in the other room if you two need to talk."

Magdalene followed after Sarah and caught her by the arm — their first touch. Sarah looked down at Magdalene's hand, then up to her eyes.

"Oh no, no, no, don't be silly," Magdalene rushed to say. Ellen watched suspiciously. Magdalene looked at Sarah but explained slowly to Ellen, "Sarah is in Olympia on a business trip, so she thinks. But that's not really why she's here."

Ellen looked at Sarah, then back at Magdalene wondering what the hell was going on.

"Well," Ellen glanced back and forth, "why *is* she here?" The exchange became increasingly surreal. Each one spoke a little too slowly.

Ellen and Magdalene looked at Sarah. Sarah glanced quickly at Ellen, laughing a little nervously, and looked at Magdalene as she said carefully, "I *am* here on a business trip."

All eyes shifted. Then Ellen asked as she furrowed her brow, "You are?"

Sarah, with animated confusion aimed at Magdalene, said, "Really, I am. That *is* what I'm doing here."

"That's what you're doing *here*?" Ellen implied disbelief.

Magdalene broke the spell and split for the stove.

Sarah hurried then to explain to Ellen, "Well, no, no, I mean I'm *here* waiting for Jean to come back. To take me to the airport. So, I'm here *now*," she looked at Magdalene who had just pulled a plastic bag with something in it from the stove, "in the meantime, meeting Magdalene." She smiled at Magdalene, strangely enamored, in spite of the awkward situation.

Magdalene flashed a devilish smile, leaned against the stove, and posed with the bag in one hand.

Ellen glanced at Magdalene, then at Sarah, and shrugged. "Whatever." And bolted to Magdalene. As she reached Magdalene, they both turned so their backs were to Sarah. Sarah watched from across the room. She couldn't see the business going on between them.

Ellen grabbed the bag from Magdalene and whispered that she'd *told* her she was going to *be* there. Ellen, in a fuss, shoved the plastic bag into her briefcase, pulled a small wad of money out, and slammed it into Magdalene's hand. Magdalene said calmly, making a big smile, "Ellen, happy face." Magdalene took a big deep breath. Ellen slapped the flap of her briefcase shut, then joined in the deep breath. In unison they turned briskly toward Sarah. All smiles.

"Well," Ellen said and shot straight for the door, Magdalene following her. "I guess I'll ... I'll ... I'll let you two get back to your ... stuff." She finished buckling her leather attaché. Buoyantly, she said, "Thanks, Magdalene —" and stopped herself from finishing the sentence. Looking at Sarah, she said, "Have a safe trip." She opened the door and left as swiftly as she had come.

Magdalene and Sarah were turned side by side as they said good-bye to Ellen. When Ellen left they turned toward each other and into an unexpected moment of intimacy that lingered momentarily. Then Sarah looked down nervously and took a step back. Magdalene went past her to the chair Sarah first sat in. Magdalene turned and leaned on it lightly. Then, with hand on her hip and a mysterious look of fun, Magdalene said, "Wouldn't you like to sit down and have some tea?"

Sarah gave in, "All right. I'll try some." And with her laptop still hanging from her, she crossed in front of Magdalene to the chair and sat.

Magdalene slid the thing off her shoulder and asked, "What's in the bag?"

"Oh, it's my computer."

"Planning on working?" Magdalene asked half laughingly and placed the case on a side table near the kitchen door.

"Yes, I am," Sarah said matter-of-factly, "I have to do a report before I get back to the office tomorrow."

Magdalene stood right next to her. "Your office in D.C.?"

"Yes," Sarah smiled and responded slowly. "That *is* where my office is." Sarah looked up at Magdalene, who seemed to have traveled off with a thought.

Magdalene looked deliberately at Sarah. "Jean and I have an open relationship." She finished her thought on the walk to the sink, "Did she tell you that?"

Sarah answered with amusement. "Actually, now that you mention it, she did." She watched Magdalene across the room. An afternoon stillness surrounded her. Colored bottles glistened in the late-day glow on the windowsill. A mixture of cut flowers, foreign to Sarah, reigned over Magdalene's counter. Magdalene seemed to unleash her thoughts out the window and into the woods as she stood in profile at the sink.

Something occurred to Sarah. She walked halfway across the room, hands in trouser pockets, and stopped. "What did you give that woman?"

Magdalene swept in front of Sarah, heading to the table with a sugar bowl. "Pot."

Sarah watched her with faint disbelief. "You sold her pot?"

Magdalene swept back in front of her to the counter. "I sold her pot," she said matter-of-factly.

Sarah watched without moving her head. "I see," she said as she blinked to herself. Then she asked, innocently looking toward Magdalene, "And Jean is okay with that?"

Magdalene swept in front of her again, this time with a teapot in hand. "Jean doesn't know."

Sarah watched Magdalene with wide eyes and a half-open mouth. Then it registered. She tossed her head back and laughed slightly at the realization. "Of course," Sarah started toward the table, "or else she'd have to lie."

Magdalene, with sassy smiling eyes, pointed quickly at Sarah, then tapped her nose. Bingo. Settled for the moment, Magdalene feasted on Sarah. Sarah sat down slowly, conscious of Magdalene's observation.

Behind Magdalene a churchlike shrine of votive candles burned. Four rows of ten red-glass holders. Most still glowed. A cherub smudged with age hung on the wall beyond her like a clock. Everywhere, were pieces of a personality. In one corner the legs of a mannequin stood upside down. A shell perched between the feet, holding a short, fat unlit candle. In front of that sat a drum, some eighteen inches in diameter, leather stretched tight, a tom-tom tied to its side. Fabric, like that on the living room windows, draped the wall near the table. On an adjacent wall hung a large colorful tapestry. The floor was wood, worn for ages, scuffed and scarred, but welcoming and comforting. The house in its entirety was small, but open and spacious feeling. It breathed in rhythm with the wild outside. Unpretentious. Unpredictable. Increasingly irresistible.

They sat near each other at the table for the moment. Then Magdalene asked, "Why do you live in D.C.?"

Sarah zeroed in on her hostess again. "I have a good job there."

"Oh, that's right." Magdalene said with a playful smirk, "You're some kind of technology big pants for some big corporation aren't you?" With that remark, Magdalene stood up and nonchalantly crossed to the counter near the sink.

This time Sarah got up and followed. "I came out to monitor a system a state agency is putting in here, to make sure it's compatible..." she paused, "with the federal system."

Magdalene sorted through tea boxes silently. She placed tea bags in a small container and went back to the table. Sat down once again and watched. It was Sarah's turn to move. A kitchen ballet was in full production.

Sarah played a moment of stillness, then glanced

111

away from Magdalene. She strolled over to an area near the kitchen door, leaned back against the wall, hands in pockets, head half down. Sarah lifted her eyes. Magdalene melted. They fused eye to eye. In a dance with destiny. One place. One time. Two souls.

A sudden shift took place. Information came to Magdalene as it sometimes did, like a hit or a bolt. She delivered it. "You really should be working for yourself."

Without moving Sarah said, "I have a great job. I'm better off working for the firm."

Magdalene held eye contact as she said, "Nine-to-five jobs will be an artifact of the twentieth century."

"An artifact!" Sarah mused. "That's good. I wish I worked nine-to-five. It's more like nine to midnight."

"Future generations will never understand," Magdalene segued into matters at hand as she headed directly toward Sarah. "After we finish our tea..." she hesitated just in front of Sarah, close enough to kiss her, "... I'll give you a treatment." She moved on to the refrigerator.

"What kind of treatment?" Sarah asked with reluctant anticipation.

"Jin shin jyutsu," Magdalene said as she closed the refrigerator door, milk in hand.

"Jin what?" Sarah asked.

Magdalene said with her back to Sarah, "Jin shin jyutsu." Magdalene opened the carton of milk and sniffed it.

Sarah's playfulness dissipated. She wheezed, and a gravity came over her. Jean was, after all, her friend. Sarah pulled out the respirator, shot herself, then approached Magdalene from the side. "I'm sorry, I really don't think I can drink the tea after all."

Magdalene barely bothered to notice Sarah's retreat. "You can skip the tea then."

"Yeah, I won't be having any. Thanks though." Sarah fixated on the stove.

"Okay, come on then, let's go in the other room."

Magdalene led Sarah to the massage table in the next room. Magdalene turned on the CD player under the eyes of the framed naked dancer and her entourage of three watching women. A tribal-sounding rhythm filled the space. The light was soft, made softer by floating fabric that flowed from a gathering point on the ceiling and spilled about the windows like a huge flower. Magdalene picked up an atomizer, misted two ferns near the door, moisturizing the air. Ceremoniously, she lit the various candles placed strategically throughout the room, gently touching the black face of the polka-dot goddess. Then she moved to the head of the bed, fluffed the pillows, billowed the bed cover.

Sarah joined the rhythmic rite, helping guide the blanket's perfect landing. Poised in the seductive shadows of enchanted ritual, Sarah's bodyguard fell under the spell, letting go its vigilant grip. Desire took hold and moved right in. The space between the two was saturated with prospect, textured with chance.

Magdalene went to Sarah, taking her by the

shoulders, turned her. Back against the bed, she slipped off Sarah's jacket, pocket respirator included, and tossed it near the window. Magdalene led Sarah in an unplanned promenade, pulling her slightly closer. Then she gently pushed Sarah's shoulders, guiding her to sit. Without losing Sarah's gaze, Magdalene dropped between Sarah's legs, slipping off her shoes. Magdalene rose again, lifted Sarah's legs onto the table, walking around the end of it. She paused a moment with her hands on Sarah's feet. Sarah was stretched before her on a daring limb of wonder, life yet to unfold. Magdalene ran her hand the length of time: up Sarah's leg, her groin, her waist, across her breast, her shoulder. They met in a breath, eye-to-eye, as Magdalene laid her back.

Sarah submitted to the setting sunlight as she relaxed into the pillow, enveloped in an enigmatic union. Magdalene's hand rested briefly but affirmingly on Sarah's shoulder. Then Magdalene slid her fingers along Sarah's arm and lifted her hand. She felt the pulse of Sarah's life: strength, and disciplined ambition. Between the pounding beats, Magdalene felt all that was hiding: abandon, trust, joy, faith in the divine.

Magdalene shifted to a stool and readied for the task. The deliberate rhythm of the pounding drums created passageways and space. She placed one hand under Sarah's back; the other on her far upper arm. Points of departure, points of pulse, points in need of equipoise. She pressed them lightly, held the pressure. Magdalene let her own body serve as the merger through which the pulse points would come into balance.

They were physically very close, Magdalene draped

across Sarah. "Can we talk while you're doing this?" Sarah asked with a mundane need to chat.
"Sure." Magdalene could easily converse.
"Are you from here?" Sarah asked earnestly.
"Oh, no."
"Where you from?"
"All over. My father was in the military," Magdalene said quietly.
"No kidding?" Sarah smiled, intoxicated with the atmosphere. "Mine, too."
Magdalene looked at Sarah with particular intimacy, lusciously close and calm. "My favorite place was Italy."
"Mine, too," Sarah said dreamily. Then she asked, "What exactly are you doing?"
"Balancing your body pulses."
"Oh, I see. Do you practice this professionally?" Sarah asked interview style.
Magdalene smiled and a spontaneous slip of a laugh came forth. "No, unprofessionally."
"I see," Sarah grinned. Bold irreverence. Sarah loved it.
Magdalene adjusted her left hand from Sarah's arm to a point just to the right of her pelvis. She smoothed out Sarah's slacks and pressed her four fingertips down flatly. An electric violin heightened the percussion track with melody; and a charged fluidity permeated the air. Sarah exhaled deeply and closed her eyes, an electric symphony surged from her. Her body vibrated... the untouched unblocked... at the hands of a woman dark and daring ... the pounding heat of energy unleashed... in the arms of woman present and powerful... the pulsating cadence of fiery desire... the rushing rhythms from a

heart unlocked, released. Her heart beat and beat, thumped and pounded. Her heart opened and flowed with the pulsating beat of life. The charge between them was unbreakable.

Sarah, opening her eyes, looked at Magdalene, whose eyes were closed. Sarah took a deep breath. Another. The resounding pulse within her was beginning to soften. Energy was running through her from head to toe like a spring river. Magdalene opened soft eyes and slowly connected with Sarah's. A sprite suddenly danced within their glance. Fairies of dust and lust sprinkled their work all through the air. And the devil of dare perched on Magdalene's shoulder. Magdalene ventured, "Sarah, may I ask you a personal question?"

Sarah affirmed with her eyes.

"What do you like?" Magdalene dared one step closer.

"What do you mean?" Sarah looked directly at Magdalene.

A dangerous smile infiltrated Magdalene's visage. Her eyebrows raised ever so slightly and her mouth opened slowly. "You like to be on top, don't you?" The music stopped.

Slowly the smile spread to Sarah as well. She diverted, "Did you have this all planned?"

"I don't believe in plans," Magdalene said fully engaged and game to follow Sarah's lead.

Sarah held Magdalene's gaze and lured her further. "What do you believe in?"

Magdalene inhaled contemplatively, then told her with lighthearted thoughtfulness, "I believe in good friends, good food, and divinity."

"You mean like predetermined destiny?"

"Oh, no," Magdalene continued the treatment as they spoke. "Predetermination is a dying concept. It deprives us of our choice," she said with matter-of-fact inspiration. "I believe in chaos" she smiled, "and spontaneity. You?"

"Oh god, I don't know," Sarah looked away from Magdalene, challenged to reflect in an unaccustomed way. She took a deep breath, eyes open but focused inward. "I believe in," she paused as the truth came to her, and grinned, "never leaving dirty dishes in the sink at night, making my bed every morning no matter how depressed I am." Magdalene was completely absorbed as Sarah went on, "And I believe," Sarah turned her head and penetrated Magdalene's eyes, "in making love all night long." Fusion.

"Oh, you do, do you?" Magdalene met her match. The sprite split. The fairy dust settled. The daredevil vanished. Magdalene withdrew her arms from under Sarah's back and from across her front. She got up and walked around the head of the table to Sarah's other side. She stood, lifted Sarah's forearm to her, put her fingers to her wrist, and rechecked her pulse.

Sarah continued the dialogue, "You don't believe in monogamy?"

Magdalene answered without hesitation, "Not at the moment." Then as the smile crept back in, "and neither do you."

"How do you know?" Sarah smirked.

"I know," Magdalene said with cryptic authority.

"What else do you *know*?" Sarah treaded slyly.

Magdalene replied furtively but directly, "You like dirty talk."

"Oh, I do?" Sarah cajoled.

"You don't like to talk dirty yourself, you like your lover to talk dirty to you," Magdalene said with flirtatious and lingering eyes. Without letting go of Sarah's gaze, she walked around the foot of the table and along the other side.

Magdalene took hold of Sarah's other wrist to check the pulse as Sarah asked, "And you, what do you like?"

Magdalene leaned closely to her and said with sultry confidentiality, "I like to talk dirty. And I like to be on the bottom."

Meltdown. Sarah met her match. Her body smiled.

Magdalene released Sarah's hand perfunctorily. "There." She walked around the head of the bed, picked up Sarah's blazer, and sat on the edge as Sarah sat up quickly to meet her.

"I've changed my mind about the tea," Sarah said decisively. "I'll try some after all." She leaned down, picked her shoes up in one hand, and stood up.

Magdalene said with a surprising touch of tentativeness, "I'd love it if you had some tea with me."

"It's never appealed to me before," Sarah said with a daredevil of her own hovering. She looked at Magdalene over her shoulder at she walked into the kitchen. She uncharacteristically dropped her shoes on the floor with abandon, put her jacket on with satisfaction, sat down at the table, and slipped on her shoes.

Magdalene meanwhile was walking from candle to candle in the living room, slowly extinguishing them. She misted the ferns and this time shot a spray above herself. Eventually, she reemerged in the kitchen and sat down in a chair next to Sarah and near the kitchen door.

Without saying anything, Sarah, with a flair, picked up the teapot, took a mug from the table, poured, and presented it to Magdalene. She took it from Sarah's hand cautiously. Sarah held that pose, smiling impetuously. Magdalene wrapped both hands safely around the mug. Then Sarah poured herself a cup of tea with equal ceremony. She placed the teapot on the table. Then relaxing, she held the mug and proceeded to gulp it in a fashion much more common to beer drinking than tea sipping. After a swallow Sarah looked deeply into the container of tea almost as if it had something to tell her. Then she looked at Magdalene and leaned toward her and said with a pleasant resolve, "This is very good tea."

Magdalene nodded with amused though anxious agreement. She sat with both hands planted firmly around the mug and the mug planted firmly on the table. She bolstered herself with an inhale and proffered an observation. "You respond very well to treatment."

"Thank you," Sarah said softly without moving or losing her lock on Magdalene. Sarah assumed the comment to be a compliment.

Magdalene continued in a clinical way, "The effects will be . . . uh . . . subtle at first . . ." A noticeable shortness of breath encroached upon her smile. Nervousness. ". . . then it will be more obvious over the next few days."

Sarah portended, "Something to look forward to."

Suddenly, the squeak of the front door swinging open intruded along with an energetic, "Hello!"

Sarah automatically leaned away from Magdalene. Magdalene went to the kitchen doorway just as a slim, energetic woman walked in, stretching her arms open to greet Magdalene with a hug. She wore a long, soft, light-brown skirt, a thin, darker brown T-shirt with an unbuttoned faded denim shirt over it. A big, paisley silk scarf with browns and golds draped about her shoulders. Golden half-moons dangled from both ears, and over her left shoulder hung a worn, brown leather bag.

"It's nice to see you! It's been so long," Magdalene gave her a warm and welcoming embrace.

"I just came by for my reading." The woman, upbeat, turned to Sarah, "Hi, I'm Grace." She reached out with crimson nails and shook Sarah's hand.

"Nice to meet you. I'm Sarah." Sarah was suddenly slightly apprehensive.

Magdalene got down to business immediately. "Have a seat, Grace," relieved at having this intrusion to focus on. She ushered Grace to the chair she'd been sitting in and walked around the table to the chair in which Sarah had first found her. Sarah watched with modest suspicion as Magdalene said, "Grace, let me hold your scarf."

Grace handed it across the table. Sarah watched Magdalene's focus shift and said, "I think I'll go in the other room and do some work."

"No, don't go," Grace touched Sarah's arm. "This is good that you're here. Really, it feels right."

Sarah acquiesced and settled back into her hard wooden chair. Magdalene noticed nothing of the exchange between the two. She was completely

absorbed elsewhere. Suddenly, she spoke to Grace, "You've got something going on with your teeth."
"Get outta here girl," Grace rejected that reality.
"You do. You need to go to a dentist immediately," Magdalene grimaced. Sarah stared intently at her as she continued, "You have a bad toothache, don't you?"
Sarah turned to Grace, watched for her response. Grace conceded, "Sure as shit I do."
"It's making *my* mouth ache." Magdalene held the scarf farther away from her body as if for relief. "You're gonna lose your tooth if you don't get to a dentist." She refocused on Grace. Sarah, too, refocused on Grace.
"Oh, man, I hate dentists," Grace said imploringly.
Magdalene unexpectedly veered to another topic. "What's with your car?" Sarah's attention jumped back to Magdalene.
"My car?" Grace asked, surprised.
Magdalene's eyes darted rapidly about. "Something's going on with your car."
Grace thought for a minute. "Nothing's going on with my car," she shook her head affirming. "Knock on wood." She tapped her knuckles on the table and smiled at Sarah. Then something occurred to her out of the blue, "Except for my goddamn horn."
"Yes," Magdalene reacted emphatically, and Sarah watched with increasing disbelief. "That's it. It's the horn."
"The damn thing honks any damn time it wants to," Grace volunteered.
Magdalene's adrenaline raced. "It's true isn't it?

Your car has been honking uncontrollably hasn't it?" She clutched Grace's scarf near her face, eyes shooting wildly about her hands.

Sarah shrugged with amusement and looked for Grace's response.

"Man, it's embarrassing," Grace said. "I took it to my mechanic, but she couldn't find anything wrong with it."

Sarah's eyes dropped into her tea mug, a crooked smile slanted her face.

Magdalene's voice got very soft. "Tell me, who's Rita?"

"Rita?" Grace pulled her hands together in front of her chest. "Rita is my sister." Seriousness painted her face. "She died three years ago."

Sarah was drawn out of the tea and back into the reading.

Then Magdalene said, "The honking — it's not a mechanical problem. It's Rita."

Sarah's eyes widened as she turned toward Magdalene. She stopped a smile in mid-spread, attempted to honor the serious moment.

"Man, whaddaya sayin'?" Grace asked.

Magdalene went on as if she were interpreting someone. "She's trying to communicate with you. She's just letting you know she's out there, and that she's okay."

Sarah's jaw fell open.

Grace leaned her elbows on the table and shook her head. "Jesus," she laughed a little. "She always did have a thing for my bug." Her eyes danced fleetingly in a memory of Rita stealing her convertible VW one Fourth of July weekend. Then she remembered the main reason she came. "Magdalene, what about my love life?"

Sarah's head swerved to Magdalene without changing planes. Only her eyes rolled, dubiously.

"Your love, life..." Magdalene whispered to herself, moving the scarf between her fingers, eyes fluttering. "Your love — you..." she winced, "... don't have the room." She shook her head negatively. Sarah's chin lowered and her eyebrows went up. She shot a quick glance at Grace and back to the reader extraordinaire. "You're still involved with someone else... who is that... a woman, a woman from the midwest," Magdalene finally said with conviction.

Sarah cracked up quietly.

"Detroit," Grace admitted.

"Yes," Magdalene exclaimed.

"The Detroit Diva," Grace said with resignation that she punctuated by mugging at the thought.

"You need to let her go once and for all."

"You're tellin' me," Grace rolled *her* eyes, disgustedly.

Magdalene went on, "You need to make room in your life for someone new." Sarah was thoroughly entertained.

Grace perked up. "Someone new?"

"Oh, yes," Magdalene continued happily. "And that someone has a... puppy." The word jumped out of her mouth completely by surprise.

"A puppy?" Grace repeated it for clarification.

"And you're gonna love that puppy," Magdalene added sweetly.

Finally, Sarah interrupted. "Does this someone have a name?"

Grace immediately acknowledged that was one good question. "I knew you were here for a reason." Then she looked to Magdalene and awaited the answer.

Magdalene dangled the scarf toward Sarah and quipped, "Well, maybe *you'd* like to do the reading, missy?"

Touché. Sarah simply smirked

Magdalene redirected her attention, "I'm sorry. I'm not getting a name right now Grace." And she handed back the scarf. "That's all I can do right now." Magdalene folded her arms together on the table and relaxed.

"That's fine," Grace giggled a little. She straightened her scarf and took a deep breath to digest it all. As she laid the fabric around her shoulders she said, "It's no wonder that I don't come here that often. It's like I love this, but it scares the shit outta me at the same time." She reached into her denim shirt pocket, pulled out some crinkled cash, and slid it across the table to Magdalene. "Be good to yourself, honey."

"Back atchya." Magdalene swept up the money and placed it in her bra.

Sarah readjusted her position in the chair as she watched Magdalene stuff the money.

Grace got up from the table, collected. She stepped in front of Sarah and put out her hand. "Nice meeting you." They shook hands.

"Good luck," Sarah looked up and said modestly.

"Hmmm," Grace hummed an approval as she onced Sarah over before leaving. Then she left the same way she'd come, closing the front door behind herself.

Sarah turned abruptly toward Magdalene. Magdalene scooted her chair from the table, sidewise, onto the same plane as Sarah's. Facing away from Sarah, Magdalene looked across the room. Sarah leaned on the table toward her. Still, they were a couple of feet apart. The brick column imposed itself ever so slightly between them. Sarah didn't take her eyes off Magdalene. And Magdalene wouldn't look at Sarah. Finally, Sarah asked, "What?"

"What do ya mean, what?" Magdalene looked at her.

"What?" Sarah asked again.

Magdalene said nothing. Sarah expected her to do or say something. Make some move toward her. She didn't. So Sarah got up, walked around the table to Magdalene. Magdalene sat still, didn't breathe until Sarah stopped in front of her and dropped down on one knee in between Magdalene's legs. Sarah was within inches of Magdalene's absorbing eyes, could smell the freshness of her neck, feel the heat of her chest, taste the sweetness of her breath, and finally she presented Magdalene with a question. "Did you *divine* this?"

The thread of destiny danced between them, pulling them closer, a heartbeat away from the kiss of a lifetime. Profoundly, inescapably attracted, they were magnetized. The lips of love opened, and the truth between them touched. The premier kiss: intense, slow and delicious.

"Come here." Sarah rose with a rush and pulled Magdalene with her. They met eye-to-eye on a new level. "You like to be told what to do, don't you?" Sarah beheld.

"I kinda love it," Magdalene's arms were about

Sarah's shoulders. Her face glowed with the beauty of openness.

"What else do you love?" Sarah led the dance daringly.

Magdalene followed bravely. "I'd love to have you inside me right now."

Slowly, intimacy began to wrap about them as Sarah vowed, "I am inside you."

Transported, they were, by a kiss, a bold and transforming kiss. Urgent lips locked in abandon, whirling into places they had never gone before. Future landscapes and lifescapes spun about them, searching souls in spontaneous ecstasy, reeling into feelings they'd never experienced before. Rapture. Magdalene flushed from Sarah's delicate touch on her face, her neck. Sarah softly slipped Magdalene's cotton shirt aside, dauntlessly kissing the secrets off her shoulder, kissing the stories behind her eyes . . . powerful, transcendent kisses . . . penetrating and blissful morsels of love.

Slowly, Sarah interrupted the moment, saying, "You're not going to believe what I have to say to you." They stood embroiled in the middle of the kitchen.

Magdalene lightly touched Sarah's lips as she responded, "Just say it."

Sarah began to relax, a smile lit as she said finally, "I gotta pee."

Magdalene leaned against her and dared, "Go ahead."

"No, I really gotta go. Where's the bathroom?"

With barely a lip of space between them yet, Magdalene slipped in a pointing finger. "Through there," she said. Sarah grabbed hold of Magdalene's hand as if to never let her go, pressed it against her chest. Magdalene's mouth brushed Sarah's gently and hotly. Whether from fear, premonition, or nature truly calling, Sarah pulled herself from the embrace and left the room.

Magdalene watched after her, and the stress of reality swelled in her. She backed away from the place of their embrace. Her hand pulled first at her chin, then at her hair as she stepped farther away from Sarah's direction. Finally she turned away. Went to the refrigerator, pulled out a small plastic bottle of water, walked over to the stove where she leaned back and drank, as if for clarity.

A mere instant of stillness was betrayed by the kitchen door. Shockingly, it swung open. Jean. Happy, alive, and innocent. Her eyes washed over Magdalene with tenderness, smiling. "Hi," she walked smoothly to Magdalene and kissed her mouth gently. "Where's Sarah?" Jean turned automatically and hung her jacket on the wall which Sarah had leaned against so deftly.

"She's in the bathroom," Magdalene gestured with contrived nonchalance.

"Did ya have fun?" Jean inquired.

"Uh huh..."

"She's somethin', huh?" Jean said, smiling over her shoulder as she headed to the refrigerator.

"Uh huh..." Magdalene obliged. Not a daredevil in sight.

Jean took out a bottle of water and asked as she turned to Magdalene, "Wanna go to the airport with us?"

Magdalene folded her arms, closing as much space around herself as possible. "I have two more clients tonight." Then she remembered to ask, "How was the test?"

Jean put the bottle down on the counter after taking a swig. "Very weird. There were about three hundred questions." She journeyed back through the test in her mind, stepped past Magdalene toward the bathroom, paused near a window, and looked away. "They asked me if I loved my mother about thirty different times."

Magdalene, barely breathing, watched Jean. Then quietly, Jean turned toward her. Jean looked at Magdalene slowly and spoke carefully, "I have a weird feeling."

Magdalene's eyes, filled with anticipation, sadness, and love, dropped momentarily to the floor, then back up to Jean. "What is it?"

Standing only inches away, Jean said, "I have a feeling... I'm really going to become a cop." She smiled, accomplished.

Magdalene searched Jean's face in disbelief. Looked at her through big brown globes bursting with information. Magdalene caved at the relief that whisked through her. "Me, too," she said with a subtle hint of apology that Jean was not attuned to.

"Thank god." Jean pulled Magdalene into an encompassing hug, relieved at her concurrence. They were fully engaged in an embrace when Sarah returned. Jean's back was to Sarah. Sarah's footsteps were light and unnoticed. Sarah watched the two briefly, stunned. And finally she interrupted, "I guess it's time."

Jean broke the hug with a wide smile cast over her shoulder toward Sarah. Jean kept an arm around Magdalene, moved to Sarah, and beckoned her their way. Jean succeeded in converging the three quickly in the middle of the room, she at the center, one arm around each. Jean beamed, "So, you got to meet!"

"We did," Magdalene confessed.

"Yes, we did," Sarah added.

The two women, caught looking at each other, both backed a step away from Jean.

"I'm really glad," Sarah confessed.

"So am I," Magdalene said too quickly.

Jean stood suspended between the two, her arms stretched out to maintain contact. She glanced from Magdalene to Sarah and back to Magdalene, rubbing Magdalene's shoulder unconsciously and rapidly. The stories in the air became thick like a blanket. Jean watched as the two women's eyes kept diverting into some strange dance with each other. The silence of the event screamed. Jean saw in Sarah's face the urge to speak, then the rush to stifle it. In Magdalene, Jean saw conclusion, her lover gone. Jean looked again at Sarah and dropped her hand. Hurt. Jean turned her eyes away from Sarah, back to Magdalene. Disbelief flooded Jean. She stood like a thin frail child, looking at Magdalene, as if to say, tell me this isn't what I think it is . . .

Magdalene held Jean with her eyes as the realization sunk in. Jean dropped her hand from Magdalene's shoulder. Betrayal. Jean recoiled for safety. Stepping back, she looked with resignation at the two. She found an escape. Jean pointed to the computer bag, "That was all you brought in, right?" Jean backed farther away, and walked widely around Magdalene to the small table by the door where the bag waited.

"Yeah, that's it, right," Sarah said slowly without moving.

Jean picked up the bag, turned, and looked directly at the two. Her eyes filled with the sudden splashes of unexpected events. Jean swallowed as she spoke, and her voice sounded strained. "I'll, uh, be out in the car." She looked at Sarah, but stepped as if unable not to, toward Magdalene. Jean took hold of Magdalene's hand and placed one sweet, familiar, unrushed kiss upon her lips. "Bye, sweetie."

Magdalene faltered in the wake of Jean's dignity. An artist of life, fully present even in chaos and spontaneity. The attraction that had once brought Jean and Magdalene together, magnified: Jean with her wide-eyed presence; Magdalene with her fearless confidence. Exchange complete. Bittersweet.

Jean backed away then, still holding Magdalene's hand, and said softly with a crack in her voice, "I'll see you in a couple of hours." She walked out quietly and closed the door behind her without demand.

Magdalene turned to Sarah who moved closer and took hold of her hands with urgency. They looked at each other, surrounded by ramifications. "I can't believe this," Sarah finally said. A part of her swirled yet in that place where they left off kissing. Magdalene met her there again. Sarah closed her eyes and said, as much to remind herself as anyone, "I really need to get home."

"I know." And Magdalene did know. "You'll be back," she pronounced unceremoniously.

"Not for a long time," Sarah guessed.

Magdalene removed her necklace, putting it carefully on Sarah. Magdalene held Sarah's face in her hands and kissed her forehead. Magdalene breathed deeply, taking Sarah by the shoulders, and said, "You'll be working for yourself within a year."

Sarah savored her soothsayer, "Oh, will I?"

Magdalene nodded, "And living with me." She smiled fleetingly at her own premonition.

Sarah's momentary playfulness scattered. "And Jean?" she asked.

Without hesitation Magdalene said, "I love Jean very, very much. But she and I will be better friends than lovers." She paused a second before divulging, then proceeded with a glint, "Besides, Jean's going to meet the love of her life in about four months."

Sarah laughed lightly, but not discountingly. "What about you?" she asked.

Magdalene set her hand over the necklace on Sarah's heart and moved into her eyes. "Baby, I've met mine."

Sarah wrapped her hand around the charm. Pulling away with effort, she managed her way to the kitchen door, opened it, and before leaving looked at Magdalene. "It's true that I'm sick of my job." She closed the door, and Magdalene watched her go... into a universe of stuff to deal with.

From the back porch, the yard looked different to Sarah. The tall laurel hedge and flowers were comforting. The wooden porch beneath her shoes was inviting. The geraniums and alyssum cascading from the eaves seemed to understand all that happened. The rhododendrons looked knowingly from their unquestionably green leaves. She stepped down from the porch and onto the red-brick walk. It greeted her like an old dog that she'd known forever. Jean, sitting in the pickup cab, came into view as Sarah approached the gate. Sarah's hand fell comfortably on the worn wood, swinging it open slowly, respectfully, but smoothly. Closing it and resting her hand on the sympathetic board, Sarah gazed back at the place she'd just been introduced to. A budding metamorphosis, wild within.

The afternoon stillness was too appropriate. Sarah turned to face the unfolding, the friendly fence behind her, Magdalene's amulet against her heart. Jean sat without looking at Sarah, hands pondered at the steering wheel. Sarah opened the passenger door and sat on the edge of the seat, uncertain. Jean only glanced at her, then stared back at the wheel. Sarah studied her first, then asked, "Do you want me to call a cab?"

Jean took the question in. Reflected. Gradually she shook her head as an unwanted smile inched at her mouth. "No," Jean said, yet offered no relief to Sarah by way of outbursts, accusations, understanding looks, or anything at all. Jean simply continued looking at her hands playing at the steering wheel. Sarah waited for a cue. Searched for something to say. Something remotely fitting. Nothing.

The environment strangely supported the moment. The sky, house, trees, flowers, birds, and distant dogs all flourished confidently under the tension.

Finally, Jean pricked the tautness. "She's a trip, huh."

The two friends sat quietly a moment, with a delicate situation to hazard, bound for discovery.

"Okay then," Sarah said, "let's go."

A few of the publications of
THE NAIAD PRESS, INC.
P.O. Box 10543 • Tallahassee, Florida 32302
Phone (904) 539-5965
Toll-Free Order Number: 1-800-533-1973
*Mail orders welcome. Please include 15% postage.
Write or call for our free catalog which also features an incredible selection of lesbian videos.*

COSTA BRAVA by Marta Balletbo Coll. 144 pp. Read the book, see the movie! ISBN 1-56280-153-8 $11.95

MEETING MAGDALENE & OTHER STORIES by Marilyn Freeman. 144 pp. Read the book, see the movie! ISBN 1-56280-170-8 11.95

SECOND FIDDLE by Kate Calloway. 208 pp. P.I. Cassidy James' second case. ISBN 1-56280-169-6 11.95

LAUREL by Isabel Miller. 128 pp. By the author of the beloved *Patience and Sarah*. ISBN 1-56280-146-5 10.95

LOVE OR MONEY by Jackie Calhoun. 240 pp. The romance of real life. ISBN 1-56280-147-3 10.95

SMOKE AND MIRRORS by Pat Welch. 224 pp. 5th Helen Black Mystery. ISBN 1-56280-143-0 10.95

DANCING IN THE DARK edited by Barbara Grier & Christine Cassidy. 272 pp. Erotic love stories by Naiad Press authors. ISBN 1-56280-144-9 14.95

TIME AND TIME AGAIN by Catherine Ennis. 176 pp. Passionate love affair. ISBN 1-56280-145-7 10.95

PAXTON COURT by Diane Salvatore. 256 pp. Erotic and wickedly funny contemporary tale about the business of learning to live together. ISBN 1-56280-114-7 10.95

INNER CIRCLE by Claire McNab. 208 pp. 8th Carol Ashton Mystery. ISBN 1-56280-135-X 10.95

LESBIAN SEX: AN ORAL HISTORY by Susan Johnson. 240 pp. Need we say more? ISBN 1-56280-142-2 14.95

BABY, IT'S COLD by Jaye Maiman. 256 pp. 5th Robin Miller Mystery. ISBN 1-56280-141-4 19.95

WILD THINGS by Karin Kallmaker. 240 pp. By the undisputed mistress of lesbian romance. ISBN 1-56280-139-2 10.95

THE GIRL NEXT DOOR by Mindy Kaplan. 208 pp. Just what
you'd expect. ISBN 1-56280-140-6 10.95
NOW AND THEN by Penny Hayes. 240 pp. Romance on the
westward journey. ISBN 1-56280-121-X 10.95
HEART ON FIRE by Diana Simmonds. 176 pp. The romantic and
erotic rival of *Curious Wine*. ISBN 1-56280-152-X 10.95
DEATH AT LAVENDER BAY by Lauren Wright Douglas. 208 pp.
1st Allison O'Neil Mystery. ISBN 1-56280-085-X 10.95
YES I SAID YES I WILL by Judith McDaniel. 272 pp. Hot
romance by famous author. ISBN 1-56280-138-4 10.95
FORBIDDEN FIRES by Margaret C. Anderson. Edited by Mathilda
Hills. 176 pp. Famous author's "unpublished" Lesbian romance.
ISBN 1-56280-123-6 21.95
SIDE TRACKS by Teresa Stores. 160 pp. Gender-bending
Lesbians on the road. ISBN 1-56280-122-8 10.95
HOODED MURDER by Annette Van Dyke. 176 pp. 1st Jessie
Batelle Mystery. ISBN 1-56280-134-1 10.95
WILDWOOD FLOWERS by Julia Watts. 208 pp. Hilarious and
heart-warming tale of true love. ISBN 1-56280-127-9 10.95
NEVER SAY NEVER by Linda Hill. 224 pp. Rule #1: Never get involved
with . . . ISBN 1-56280-126-0 10.95
THE SEARCH by Melanie McAllester. 240 pp. Exciting top cop
Tenny Mendoza case. ISBN 1-56280-150-3 10.95
THE WISH LIST by Saxon Bennett. 192 pp. Romance through
the years. ISBN 1-56280-125-2 10.95
FIRST IMPRESSIONS by Kate Calloway. 208 pp. P.I. Cassidy
James' first case. ISBN 1-56280-133-3 10.95
OUT OF THE NIGHT by Kris Bruyer. 192 pp. Spine-tingling
thriller. ISBN 1-56280-120-1 10.95
NORTHERN BLUE by Tracey Richardson. 224 pp. Police recruits
Miki & Miranda — passion in the line of fire. ISBN 1-56280-118-X 10.95
LOVE'S HARVEST by Peggy J. Herring. 176 pp. by the author of
Once More With Feeling. ISBN 1-56280-117-1 10.95
THE COLOR OF WINTER by Lisa Shapiro. 208 pp. Romantic
love beyond your wildest dreams. ISBN 1-56280-116-3 10.95
FAMILY SECRETS by Laura DeHart Young. 208 pp. Enthralling
romance and suspense. ISBN 1-56280-119-8 10.95
INLAND PASSAGE by Jane Rule. 288 pp. Tales exploring conventional & unconventional relationships. ISBN 0-930044-56-8 10.95
DOUBLE BLUFF by Claire McNab. 208 pp. 7th Carol Ashton
Mystery. ISBN 1-56280-096-5 10.95

BAR GIRLS by Lauran Hoffman. 176 pp. See the movie, read
the book! ISBN 1-56280-115-5 10.95
THE FIRST TIME EVER edited by Barbara Grier & Christine
Cassidy. 272 pp. Love stories by Naiad Press authors.
ISBN 1-56280-086-8 14.95
MISS PETTIBONE AND MISS McGRAW by Brenda Weathers.
208 pp. A charming ghostly love story. ISBN 1-56280-151-1 10.95
CHANGES by Jackie Calhoun. 208 pp. Involved romance and
relationships. ISBN 1-56280-083-3 10.95
FAIR PLAY by Rose Beecham. 256 pp. 3rd Amanda Valentine
Mystery. ISBN 1-56280-081-7 10.95
PAYBACK by Celia Cohen. 176 pp. A gripping thriller of romance,
revenge and betrayal. ISBN 1-56280-084-1 10.95
THE BEACH AFFAIR by Barbara Johnson. 224 pp. Sizzling
summer romance/mystery/intrigue. ISBN 1-56280-090-6 10.95
GETTING THERE by Robbi Sommers. 192 pp. Nobody does it
like Robbi! ISBN 1-56280-099-X 10.95
FINAL CUT by Lisa Haddock. 208 pp. 2nd Carmen Ramirez
Mystery. ISBN 1-56280-088-4 10.95
FLASHPOINT by Katherine V. Forrest. 256 pp. A Lesbian
blockbuster! ISBN 1-56280-079-5 10.95
CLAIRE OF THE MOON by Nicole Conn. Audio Book —Read
by Marianne Hyatt. ISBN 1-56280-113-9 16.95
FOR LOVE AND FOR LIFE: INTIMATE PORTRAITS OF
LESBIAN COUPLES by Susan Johnson. 224 pp.
ISBN 1-56280-091-4 14.95
DEVOTION by Mindy Kaplan. 192 pp. See the movie — read
the book! ISBN 1-56280-093-0 10.95
SOMEONE TO WATCH by Jaye Maiman. 272 pp. 4th Robin
Miller Mystery. ISBN 1-56280-095-7 10.95
GREENER THAN GRASS by Jennifer Fulton. 208 pp. A young
woman — a stranger in her bed. ISBN 1-56280-092-2 10.95
TRAVELS WITH DIANA HUNTER by Regine Sands. Erotic
lesbian romp. Audio Book (2 cassettes) ISBN 1-56280-107-4 16.95
CABIN FEVER by Carol Schmidt. 256 pp. Sizzling suspense
and passion. ISBN 1-56280-089-1 10.95
THERE WILL BE NO GOODBYES by Laura DeHart Young. 192
pp. Romantic love, strength, and friendship. ISBN 1-56280-103-1 10.95
FAULTLINE by Sheila Ortiz Taylor. 144 pp. Joyous comic
lesbian novel. ISBN 1-56280-108-2 9.95
OPEN HOUSE by Pat Welch. 176 pp. 4th Helen Black Mystery.
ISBN 1-56280-102-3 10.95

ONCE MORE WITH FEELING by Peggy J. Herring. 240 pp.
Lighthearted, loving romantic adventure. ISBN 1-56280-089-2 10.95
FOREVER by Evelyn Kennedy. 224 pp. Passionate romance — love
overcoming all obstacles. ISBN 1-56280-094-9 10.95
WHISPERS by Kris Bruyer. 176 pp. Romantic ghost story
ISBN 1-56280-082-5 10.95
NIGHT SONGS by Penny Mickelbury. 224 pp. 2nd Gianna Maglione
Mystery. ISBN 1-56280-097-3 10.95
GETTING TO THE POINT by Teresa Stores. 256 pp. Classic
southern Lesbian novel. ISBN 1-56280-100-7 10.95
PAINTED MOON by Karin Kallmaker. 224 pp. Delicious
Kallmaker romance. ISBN 1-56280-075-2 10.95
THE MYSTERIOUS NAIAD edited by Katherine V. Forrest &
Barbara Grier. 320 pp. Love stories by Naiad Press authors.
ISBN 1-56280-074-4 14.95
DAUGHTERS OF A CORAL DAWN by Katherine V. Forrest.
240 pp. Tenth Anniversay Edition. ISBN 1-56280-104-X 10.95
BODY GUARD by Claire McNab. 208 pp. 6th Carol Ashton
Mystery. ISBN 1-56280-073-6 10.95
CACTUS LOVE by Lee Lynch. 192 pp. Stories by the beloved
storyteller. ISBN 1-56280-071-X 9.95
SECOND GUESS by Rose Beecham. 216 pp. 2nd Amanda Valentine
Mystery. ISBN 1-56280-069-8 9.95
A RAGE OF MAIDENS by Lauren Wright Douglas. 240 pp. 6th Caitlin
Reece Mystery. ISBN 1-56280-068-X 10.95
TRIPLE EXPOSURE by Jackie Calhoun. 224 pp. Romantic drama
involving many characters. ISBN 1-56280-067-1 10.95
UP, UP AND AWAY by Catherine Ennis. 192 pp. Delightful
romance. ISBN 1-56280-065-5 9.95
PERSONAL ADS by Robbi Sommers. 176 pp. Sizzling short
stories. ISBN 1-56280-059-0 10.95
CROSSWORDS by Penny Sumner. 256 pp. 2nd Victoria Cross
Mystery. ISBN 1-56280-064-7 9.95
SWEET CHERRY WINE by Carol Schmidt. 224 pp. A novel of
suspense. ISBN 1-56280-063-9 9.95

These are just a few of the many Naiad Press titles — we are the oldest and largest lesbian/feminist publishing company in the world. We also offer an enormous selection of lesbian video products. Please request a complete catalog. We offer personal service; we encourage and welcome direct mail orders from individuals who have limited access to bookstores carrying our publications.